CHRONOLOGICAL ORDER

CHRONOLOGICAL ORDER

MARIO SAVIONI

CONTENTS

UNSCHEDULED EVENT

1988

At home, I shiver while winds run into louvers, like trains through corridors in a government building. The temperature is 65ºF, chilly for Hawaii. It requires a thick coat to keep warm and a family of friends sitting on a long couch in a damp house, where raindrops and termites work together to provide the water spotting on the black and white tiles.

This is the second day of freak weather, worse than Hurricane Iwa. It rains so hard you can't reach the island's Eastside from the North or South. In some places, the water reaches five feet, and furniture floats. Cars flood, and some press against landslides, filling highway lanes as rain gushes across them.

Teenagers having fun in darkness pull bicycles in waist-deep water on the Waimanalo side past the point only Mac trucks can go. We watch water sputter from our exhaust pipe, a collection tube in this weather, and flooding. My wife and I drive to the Nui Valley roadblock, where drivers sneak along the highway on the left and find the depth too deep by car or truck. Confused, we wait, imagining an accident as the fire engine horns blare. Waiting for a half-hour, we steal alongside the streets... We are late for a New Year's Eve party in Hawaii Kai.

Where Nuuanu Pali Road and Pali Highway meet, we ask an officer how we can get to Hawaii Kai. He says we can probably go by way of Likelike Highway. Near Kailua, we drive alongside a Mercedes as the rain rushes through our wheels in a soft brown, after which a landslide ocurs in my lane. The engine cools, and the carburetor is flooded for twenty minutes. It is dark and unfriendly. Cars line the highway, but where are the people? I see a woman without a raincoat trying to reach a police car; she hesitates. She decides against it and disappears into the darkness. Trying the vehicle, we are along the railing. We might be comfortable except we have a party to go to. It is 12:30 AM. The car starts. Driving slowly is my wife's request. While crossing the Waimanalo Bridge, water is up to our doors.

Pulling into the 7-11 near Castle Hospital, we have dinner. I ate barbecue beef, orange juice, and an ice cream sandwich.

It is 3:30 PM, and we are waiting in our apartment as the rain and wind rush outside, moving like a train against the covered windows or down the roadway between the buildings. Weather forecasters are nonchalant, ignorant of the devastation. Unable to get to their parties, people shiver in their homes, seeking sympathy from regular-scheduled programming.

COMMON VOICES

January 23, 2014
If you don't love, no one will remember you.
In the orange glow of morning
No words will be spoken.
Against the back walls of yellow
You will watch the sunrise.
Reality is a sore spot for lovers.
It is the place where they make decisions.

II
I am rolling in the ocean, a small suite in the sea. Bubbly white waters cover me. The sun is ninety degrees. I hear whispers. I see shadows. Don't revive me. I am still. Listening here, I hear the ocean's voices, deep and still. There is a language we can speak. Every creature speaks to us. We are snake charmers; we are conductors. Every animal has its voice. They stand before us. They ask for music; they ask for love.

III
A single instrument well-played speaks of the capacity of a woman to go straight to the heart. The heart doesn't need

peripheral instruments. It hears a perfect set of notes and doodles on them floating in the space of self-reflection. Self-reflection is contingent upon the melody, most like the beat of this particular heart. I close my eyes and can hear a spiritual friend. We are lovers, intimate, and that is why, I think, there are stalkers. Such people run to stars, assuming they have something in common. And what they do not, or may not know, is that all of us can listen to the muse, who gives us our instrumentation or voices, and they work from inside.

IV

This common weed, the unraveled self's intricate inter-weaving, the cumulus clouds' brown moss, and Herringbone predicaments confide with light and leaves. Wishes filled this afternoon that innocence could barely feel, stared at, and dis-appointing display of the temporary advertisement. If only for the truth, I break sticks at my feet and point my eyes. I have no right, no wherefore. It is unfair to be here and not someone she could love.

I was separated in time by the economics of beauty. The calculated use of some gift, which not all women have, is a selfish instrument of God. She raises her hands because I asked her and because of the expectation, "I am on sale here, a common weed in lovers' brains or not. There is no discrimination. I am seen the same way by men and women of all ages. I represent the very center of the earth, and all the world revolves around me. I am healthy only in the sense that this is my time. Do I choose knowledge? Do I choose to wield this power? All I see is how it makes others feel. I am not this body. Like anyone, I desire to create where a whisper states my purpose. And that whisper comes from a source with no other ambition than to tell me the stories I tell you."

HEAVEN IS NOW

<u>*February 1, 2014*</u>
God is an invention
That we project on the world
Out of fear of the unknown.
What happens to us is
The by-product of our ambitions
And the ambitions of others,
Who are working within
A system of experience
And present desire.
While we get better at playing the
Game, we also get older.
Eventually, our bodies.
Fall apart, and our brains fail.
At the point of death,
We lose consciousness
And there is nothing more.

THE BELL TOWER

February 3, 2014

It happened in a suite at the top of a building with little areas dotting the luxurious but otherwise spare penthouse apartment.

In the room, various individuals were standing and talking to each other. When I passed one, a man stood above what appeared to be his belongings, and his name was Tom. He was taller, a bit red-faced, and overweight. He wore a plaid, long-sleeved Pendelton. He was balding, but I could tell his hair was brown. He looked at me as I approached the group but continued his conversation: "As an entire country, we are being brain-washed within the confines of mass media. We've been told what to believe and how to look at the world. Although our eyes, ears, and mouths differ, we are controlled and brought to the same conclusions. My belief in God was laid across my brain as an early teething blanket destined to calm my great fears where I knew I needed my mother and father."

There were beds, mattresses on the floor, a lamb's skin throw rug, and a little lamp on the base. You had to be careful when stepping through the obstacle course of these belongings. It was like a dorm room for adults. It turned out that the people were living there. Total strangers had come together with barely any belongings, and they would have parties and invite other strangers. I noticed a packet of candy with my name on it and a list of email addresses of people I knew. Someone had printed them on my computer and then handed them as if I were the party's host.

Tom continued speaking: "My mother asks in her late age why she's still in the hospital, and I tell her it is because of her Alzheimer's and that is because she never used the mathematical side of her brain. And now, she's further indoctrinated by the television, which provides her with a conservative view of everything. It doesn't matter because television stations are fine if they sell fear. After all, the products will be sold as the answer to their loss of safety and control, but then we are never really in control...."

Mark, someone I know from the past, says: "All of them were part-time workers, working at various companies, but the idea of harvested email addresses connects us. They would have dinner and even sex together in this seeming business financial district frat house of temporarily employed people. I looked out the windows and one-way mirrors and saw a man who seemed to be running from something. He had the demeanor of a purse-snatcher, and I watched what appeared to be a chase being carried out on the roof as I looked through the windows.

Tom says: "We wake up in the morning and run to work, and the guinea pig wheel houses us nicely. We see very little of the outside world, and while it isn't quite like us, the same strictures are still leading it."

Some in his group look at him and nod, while others watch the man on the roof getting caught by men with suits and Secret Service-like earplugs. They stop him quickly. Just one guy, a normal-seeming guy, grabs his arm and suspends him in pain.

Mark tells me there are many living arrangements, where people work for a temp agency and move from a temp job to a temp job, and they house these stables of business types who are just regular people with no extended families. They have no contacts other than these temporary "friends." They have no health care, no accumulated wealth, just what's around their feet. They live daily and only know their next job once they get a slip of paper the night before indicating where they'll be heading in the morning.

"Capitalism is the Elephant in the room," Tom continues, "and the psychopathic conquerors are unavoidable in their destructive tendencies."

I wondered, by Tom's conversation, why he was so antagonistic toward the set-up. It seemed comfortable. A few nights ago, I watched my love climb under a freeway overpass and into the arms of a muscle-bound man who gave me dirty looks as he moved her into the darkness, where he had a filthy mattress and heaps of garbage. It was clear she and I were over. After the earthquake, I'd lost the 5-plex in Berkeley, tagged for demolition. I still had $699,000 due on the mortgage. I'd lost my job. I was grateful to have found these people.

The set-up reminded me of Slavoj Zizek's idea, where he said that Jewish people were the only group maintaining their heritage and practices to the letter. In contrast, others seemed to have disbanded, and as a result of this, these 'individuals' had no common characteristics except this worker pool atmosphere. It reminded me of the Chinese dorm rooms at the companies that made Apple products who lived in bunk rooms but didn't know each other, and yet they worked long hours and slept inches from each other. They were fed in cafeteria-like environments and dressed alike.

I could hear Tom in the background: "In fact, that's what we can continue to look forward to: the eyes and glare of the psychopath taking out his rage that his father was never there to help his mother care for the family and now the self-destruction is certain - if you breed destruction yourself, destruction as a nation, as a world..." I stopped listening to Tom for a second.

I felt a tinge of sadness. I believed that we needed to help each other. Still, I never imagined that this would be done akin to slavery, where the worker paid his wages for a space on the floor, and they were trapped but certainly equal on this level to all the other people. But you could tell someone owned the suite, and someone was organizing us or at least garnering the benefit of our desperation and loneliness.

"This is the end we should expect," Tom said. "If it is every-man-for-himself, then the families have no chance. If it is that the strange shall survive and the weak perish, then that's all that's left."

The crows outside reminded me of the precarious state where the whole country looked over a cliff. Organization as we know it will be fundamentally broken. Kaypacha, an Internet-based astrologer, said in 2013, "Why doesn't everyone just go bankrupt?" They had. What's left when you still have to eat and sleep? I remembered the idea that our savings is our freedom, which Bejan would say when I was waiting tables before the 5-plex and the earthquake.

Tom said, "I don't see a happy ending, wherein the back of all the action is the inevitable personality of our nation, of people in general, a kind of *Lord-of-the-Flies* system of doing things.

"Look at ourselves; what makes up our day? Tom said. "What are we constantly thinking? Is it intimacy, the desire to be close to someone to share our fears, and the efforts we must instill to deceive ourselves into making it? We are exhausted and focused, with blinders on, but there's no other way but controlled acquisition and mergers with the intent of a deluded status of self-sufficiency and independence. Are our hearts no longer the organ making the world sunny, or is it for men only the desire to penetrate and for women to receive and then manipulate the sacrifice of another person by guilt for their self-preservation? And yet love makes us give everything, we think, for a greater good, but that good is only slavery? After all, we are trained so well that if we don't do what they say, we are terrorists, and they'll lock us up?" Tom questioned.

"We are reacting to the inevitable pressures upon us as 'desiring machines' in the middle of a life cycle. Let us go into the other room and make babies, and let the next generation do what we did as a second of pleasure," Tom said.

"Even the criminal knows this pattern, and I believe they call this life," Tom concluded.

THE ELEVATOR

February 10, 2014
With the shifting of the building
Given various weather scenarios,
I noticed this evening how the
The elevator button glowed red.
I waited and then pressed the button.
It was warm,
Like the hood of the car of a cheating husband.
I pressed it again but waited no longer
Looking over the railing for insensitive
Movers.
There were none.
I listened and waited.
Finally, I pushed the elevator door,
Which moved inward, and the
Elevator descended.
It rested on the ground floor,
What does a bored or frustrated person call it?
I pressed the button again, and
The elevator rose to the top.
I got in and made sure.

I shut the door.
I noticed the gap was snug,
And then it descended.

RECLUCIVITY OF SILENCE

March 5, 2014
The reclusivity of silence alone in a room;
The woman on a white pedestal is naked and posing.
I don't remember what I said to her,
But she is in agreement
Her body and effects are
The stuff of artistry.
A picture of a naked woman,
Not that we are there yet,
But this must be the arrangement,
Sets adrift so many passions.
The mystery is the biggest one.
Lost in the design itself,
My attraction,
My mind-numbing infatuation
With this character study.
Just as Picasso said:
He was only and always painting himself.
I am taking a picture of everything I've ever wanted

While wanting to know if the passion is shared
And what it might mean.
I sense she is only contemplating her appointment,
How the stool might not be that comfortable,
If the image winds up on the Internet,
And some guy like me would find it.
She's thinking about lunch,
Her studies,
Her boyfriend,
The cause of art,
The purpose of her life.
I don't think that women ever
Think of themselves as objects of beauty,
As the purpose for living that men attribute to them.
But they stand for something.

THE LIFE OF THE LAND IS PERPETUATED IN RIGHTEOUSNESS

March 6, 2014

Is it righteousness or regret that we contemplate? Is there a bucket list or a mere acceptance that the quality of life is so diminished over time that we understand the demise of our physicality? I watch my mother capitulate to the last waves that wash over her breaking body; how we can predict the steps to her final resting place, someone who was once our equal and, before that, the first beauty to have shown her face, and by whom I measure all lovers?

Tonight, I held the head of a woman with a skull like my mother's, and I massaged her. I breathed her "essential oils" through her thinning hair and followed the lines of her delicate hands as I traveled them. She leaned against me, and I felt my heart. We looked at pictures of my mother when she was 18.

Sadly, I doubt this woman loves me, and so it is. Death is

an acceptance of the truth, and like the arms flailing in the sand, it is a kind of suffocation we felt when we were born: Ua Mau Ke Ea o ka 'Āina I ka Pono.

And so perhaps you are correct: Ashes to ashes, dust to dust.

MISSED CALL

March 8, 2013
I know nothing but the quiet.
In the night
Having gone to the unit
Where a woman lives.
Outside, a man was smoking a cigarette.
When I called after having texted,
Someone hung up and turned off the lights.
I heard the dog's chain,
Then I drove away.
When I awoke
The sun was shining,
A message was sent.
She had "miscalled" me and then went to sleep.
But it wasn't her argument that persuaded me.
It was the fact that when I picked up the phone
She was talking to a woman
Reading my message and
Getting angry that I assumed
The man was hers,
When all she did was go to bed early.

Still, the drama in all of this
That is what makes it so tedious.
I am not in love,
Or if I should be
I don't feel it.
But who am I after all these years?
I am not in the running for what I want.
I am an old man living the flirtations of the past.
When I wake up tomorrow
I will be too old to consider dating as an option.
We laugh about the old having such ambitions.
There comes a time when two people
No longer look credible holding each other.

LIGHTNESS OF
BEING

March 26, 2014
I want to thank the person responsible
For the new washers.
It is not like the old ones were broken.
I bet they were loaded favoring one side
And the redistribution, as you know
In rugby, once the man with the ball
Is captured, a heap is formed.
But I don't know,
I have never really had a relationship
With the washers.
I did, however, put the coins in first
And then let the water fill,
Followed by detergent,
Let it churn a bit before
I put on clothes.
My aunt taught me
"To dilute the detergent."
Now, you start with the detergent,

Then the clothes,
Then the quarters,
It's kind of like getting your money's worth
In the beginning.
I like how it is a bowl
And nothing starts until a quarter
Is put inside.
The water fills, and the clothes are
Kept in a container so that
They both soak and get churned.
It is a rich process.
In the beginning
There is silence, then
The lockdown.
I like all the colored buttons and lights.
I like white porcelain.
It all seems so robotic.
And I have grown to like that.
That and dishes,
They are like the last things
We have to do
Before everything becomes
Automatic.
I am not even worried about the rain
Or viruses or wars
Because we live in a laundry room,
Where we have a sofa,
A bookshelf and a
Garden outside.
Let's install a shower.

And a kitchen.
As I said, however,
Once we figure out how to do the laundry
Without actually having to do it,
Which is actually like doing the dishes
In a dishwasher,
What's left?

A DREAM

April 7, 2014
I love this painting.
There is a man/woman in a trench coat,
She is wearing a watch with her hand
In a pocket,
Behind the door.
She could be a call girl with her
Pimp in the background,
Or just a beautifully wrought woman
Contemplating her power or burdens,
Someone separated, perhaps, from
Her effect on the world
Co-mingled with the fact of just being.
This image speaks to me of
What a woman must do in a world of men,
She is selling her wares,
Submitting herself to the desire to be
Lithe and luxuriously at peace.
What is she thinking?
My mother was once this beautiful,
She always seemed to be oblivious.

She thought not of men but of designs
On paper, oil paint, and how the world worked,
Wanting to change in her later years, junk
Into things of beauty.
She would contemplate,
Smoke her cigarettes and look out from her balcony
At the hillside, which grew from under her
And then up almost to a point
You could not see the sky unless you bent down
When you were sitting.
She said an uncle raped her,
And that she was forced to live with foster parents
Because in the '30s, with her father dead
When she was two and with two brothers,
Her mother could not afford to take care of her.
When her mother died, my mother said that
She was hours away, and her mother died alone.
She never wanted that to happen to her,
So she kept us close.
When she got her first commercial art job,
She walked in with a bandbox look.
They hired her out of all the prospects.
Just out of art school at CAL,
She presented a few pieces.
Then one of her bosses raped her.
My aunt said that she took off a couple of times
And my father, a doctor, had to take care of us.
All I am sure she did was go to a place
Where she could think.
How do I know this?

I am like her.
We dream a lot.
We have our drinks, but non-alcoholic,
We don't like to dull the powers of our minds.
I, too, have stared into the distance
Traveled through memories
And met loved ones.
Mainly lovers and their sleek lines,
How they made me feel and
When will we meet again
That is all I think,
In the meantime,
I make beautiful things
Like peacock feathers
To enter them.

"WHERE COLOR IS SWALLOWED"

<u>*August 20, 2014*</u>

In a bakery in Berkeley, I constructed a personal zine, a typewriter working, a cutting board in front of me, colored pens, and a table with a red and white tablecloth—drawing pads for paper zines. There are reference books for zine-making, but the thoughts of creating are maudlin.

Evidenced further by the phone call from my sister saying the dentist will be coming to my mother's nursing home within the hour, I tell my sister that I am in Berkeley beginning a zine.

It would be embarrassing to leave at this point, not to mention the ride back. The fact is that I doubt that even with me there, my sister will allow them to inflict pain on her, although her teeth are abscessed. Taking more pain to eliminate the pain at hand makes no sense. It's 4:10 p.m.

I've been here for two hours. I felt guilty and had already called back to say I would try to make it. They haven't called back. I realize they are doing me a favor. My sister wished they had known, given incident after incident, that my mother would not allow anyone to help her even for things that aren't painful and even explaining that she hears you but then forgets what you said and what the doctor said. It circulates until you give up. The doctors have refused to run tests, etc. Amazingly, they could put screws in her hip when she fell and broke it. I am worried about her slow demise but am also willing to abandon my potential need to attempt a zine on my day off.

There are 11 of us in the room—some cut pictures from books, some write with pens, and some talk. One is drinking from a cup. One is drawing. One already constructed a zine, a book about the crazy on Seinfeld getting money. The crafter did it with stamp letters and drew a perfect portrait of Kramer. It turns out it was a stamp. There are stamps of skateboards, a stamp of Saturn, candies, and date stamps for a day months ago. A compilation of a woman with a rifle and a line of children is Darsh's first zine of the day.

A man enters the bakery from the back door and wants a cranberry bar. The bakery is closed. He gets one, and someone else wants one. They complete the transactions. The music is still playing. The singer is Waxahachie, like Ani DiFranco, whom I listened to while driving to and from Seattle. Then the music stops. Isabel's drawn a woman in a long dress with the sun behind her.

I am afraid to ask the others what they are doing if I disturb them. They mentioned someone older than most of them outside who invited them. "No," Isabel said, "I thought this wouldn't interest her as something kids would do."

I still need to learn how to construct a zine. I've done books, but I have this aversion to borrowing others' images and photocopying them from books. My books have either been photo books or poetry books.

The woman in front of me constructs a hexaflexagon and gives it. I almost broke it, not knowing there was a method for opening and closing it. She shows me. I still don't get it. I am in the wrong place at the wrong time. Do you know what it feels like day after day to be in a place where you don't belong? Even my passion is work. Things I love to do are so tricky that I become distracted by them, moving on to the next, never being very good at anything, and always seeming to end on a sour note. Imagine everything ending on a sour note.

I fan through a *Flash Art* magazine issue. On the cover is a picture of Kai Althoff performing "Frausus." The problem is May-June 2002, Vol. XXXIV.

A girl, the Hexaflexagon, is getting creeped out by me. I am just writing, but she's stopped being productive and looks over at me like I am a spy or that I am not doing what I am supposed to, but I am trapped here feeling that if I left now, I would have been found out for not having anything to say. I am an observer who does not participate. I do not make things. I circulate in my mind in an unproductive state of sentimental feelings about being frozen in my own time and no one else's.

The typewriter keeps typing. Someone is making progress. About twenty with perfect posture, a young girl works magically on a book, sewing the pages with twine. She doesn't think about me except as a good spirit. I don't sense uncertainty from her, perhaps because she has a plan and carries it out. I heard somewhere, by an insane man, that you remain suspended in space if you judge others. You exact a curse against yourself. The young girl and her boyfriend are leaving. I guess because, as he said, he doesn't know how to draw, and in this manner, I might assert in a way that implies it is a discipline.

Before this, a woman who slipped into the room and who I barely looked at for fear of intruding dropped her blank-paged book in front of me and began writing. She's handsome and lean, gets a pastry, and continues writing. She is wearing a tank top and has hair under her arms. It appears she is taking the same methodological journey that I am. Researching that, at least for me, seemed overwhelming at the moment. The music is sad and melancholy; women's voices are like traveling along the highways and byways.

One of the primary cooperators says: "Did she leave because she couldn't handle the zine thing? It's just writing your thoughts."

I ask him, "Is that what it is?"

He shrugs like I am critical, but the statement is valid.

I am thinking of continuing.

In terms of age, an older woman about my age explained to the man, who may have thought I was critical. She walks around in slow, careful steps to find her way in the quagmire of uncertainty. At least, it is this way for me.

Isabel's sister comes in and quickly begins typing.

The older woman has gotten a pastry. We constantly reward ourselves before we sit down to work.

Isabel says, "They show their boobs and then get a necklace." I turn my head and look at her. The older woman takes a seat to learn what seems so foreign. She sweetens Isabel, who says the older woman's book is one of her favorites.

The music in the background is banjo and female singing. It tells of a time and place. I am not putting anything together but negativity.

"I don't know what I want to write about," Isabel's sister says.

I don't know what I want to write about either.

One man plans to interview people about what they have in their pockets.

The older woman has since left. I assume it is because of the commitment. The man who is interested in pockets has returned from a dinner break. He is on his computer, drafting a document, perhaps for his zine. Then he is gone. The commitment got to him, too. He had a significant next step, except I later saw him toward the window talking to a girl on her computer, who didn't seem to be participating. She was attractive, and he looked at me like I knew why he might be asking her questions. This was his way of being able to talk to her.

I described to Isabel's mother and grandmother in a book I read that a fetish is an object one can handle or worship far from the person infatuated. I was talking about Wilhelm Stekel's book, *Sexual Aberrations.*

His eyes met mine as I looked back toward the man interested in pockets. We are on opposite sides of the room, which confirms what I was thinking, yet I would be curious to know what he was thinking and his motivations for talking to her. I have been trying to sit next to women in cafes or public places. Otherwise, there is simply no natural way to strike up a conversation. When closer to them, you can find something to say when something happens.

I look away from him, trying to leave him to his privacy. It would be rude or hypocritical since I am doing the same thing. I am looking for intimacy and love. I am looking for someone I can go off into the world that I want, warmly and profoundly fulfilling. Instead, I am lonely here; many others can see and feel it.

I comment on the woman across from me, the lean one with hair under her arms. She seems to have prepared for her appearance. I am looking at her book full of ink drawings. It turns out she is re-engaging with a project she abandoned. It is about a man she knows who is incorporating acorns in chocolate. I tell her she should use the finished product as a commercial for him, and she raises her eyebrows but is silent like that was her idea. She says a few words confirming this, and I contemplate the application as the drawing method of advertising. I see the associative infomercials that employ a dry-erase board and a man with a dubbed and sped-up voice who talks while he draws to keep people interested.

I want to tell the truth, but I am afraid of the implications. Maybe others feel this way. What do I want to say on a given day except how stressed I am and that I don't think I can last another year at my job? My separated shoulder hurts, and I continuously wake when I sleep and never rest. I have canker sores in my mouth from where the dentist poked me when she cleaned me. My lip is sore, and I bit my lip several days ago.

The woman across from me is writing a comment about her friend using acorn flour in chocolate.

I make contact with Isabel, who is indeed running the show. She types while paying attention to her sister, who is talking and organizing, and earlier said that she didn't know what she wanted to write. Isabel meets my eyes even before I have looked. There's that telekinetic communication that seems significantly perked between genders. She doesn't condemn me but smiles warmly.

I feel uncomfortable having a purpose, trying to push myself to complete the task, and listening to other people's lives.

I don't have one of my own.

One woman talks about her house on the fault line along with the other's comment about homes that shimmy; this woman wonders about me.

Typing makes no statement unless read. She appears to be onto something through the conversation with Isabel's sister.

The one who wonders – Flexahexagon – is busy on a more significant construct. Perhaps one will describe her story, where every petal will prove flexible in making sense. I told her it would be like a Sylvia Plath poem, but she didn't hear me. She looked at me with glassy eyes.

"Does someone have the triangle stickers?"

Two are talking about a Portland trip, both for different weddings.

I ended up talking to someone whose name I forgot, a critical theorist who thinks about permission in a sexual sense.

Isabel did zines with her mother, her grandmother sitting beside me said. Her grandmother is wearing a long-sleeved red blouse drawing with colored pencils and tape that she removed. Her picture is complex lines of orange, red, and green.

Once she peeled the tape, it took on a magical form.

Isabel's mother is the daughter of the woman sitting next to me – Judy, whom they call 'Day.'

I talk to Isabel's grandmother about divorce and children, whom I don't have. The music changes from a live pianist to more female voices. Isabel's mother talks about having just helped her sister move.

One man eats his pizza, moving a slice back and forth like a harmonica over his open mouth. The wandering woman is behind the bakery case in her glasses and sucking on her lollipop, looking over the scene. Although I am not telepathic, I feel she is seeing and feeling.

Isabel's grandmother, a calligrapher for LA County, makes me feel better.

When I asked if I could publish the picture I took of 'The Wonderer,' she said no.

Meanwhile, it would appear that she's right about us; we who have thoughts of our own, and maybe like me, need to get out of ourselves. She represents a type of person, an enemy, who quashes my ability to tell the truth, no matter how hideous.

What are we all here to say? Are we here to be critical of others, to see and quash the ugly truth in ourselves?

Judy/Day writes:

"Within the soft heart lies

Colorless thorns — blunt in perception:

Dull or pointed thru trees — clouds —

Where the air is thin, where color is

swallowed."

The Hexaflexagon said she never finishes anything, where doing so was problematic. I watch her draw flowers, and they seem complete; as you know, anything removed must not have a beginning or end.

It is merely asking for permission when you assume the answer is no.

ANCIENT ROAD

September 12, 2014

I stumbled upon you. You were looking out over the water, and I asked what you were looking at, and you said Time. Every ripple, you said, represented a relationship with Time. Awareness went out across the distance, which was everything you said—the light pattern of knowing, feeling, and being. The sky was blue, the plants were green, and everything in between had the mark of a man. That interference reminded us of our effect unless the emptiness that exists without us traps. Like you, I prefer to look across the water or "The Ancient Road" and see almost no evidence of our being. We seldom do as well as Mother Nature.

My mother is sitting next to me in her wheelchair and loves music. She said it takes us outdoors. She has Alzheimer's. She can stay in the moment, but at times, like this evening, she keeps repeating this male friend I know, but I haven't a male friend that she has seen in the last couple of days, so it is eerie. She talks about a cinematic project I am working on, laying out the logistics, but I am not working on a film. The sliding glass door of my apartment is open, and we have been sitting, looking out as the sun was shining, and that was long ago. I washed her feet, trimmed her nails, and brought her coffee. We ate tortilla chips, salsa, grapes, then fried tofu. I am about to take her back to the nursing home, and she continues to talk about how the music is like going out into the country into the deep woods.

PERHAPS IT HAS ENDED

October 8, 2014

I've been using WordPress for a few years, and while it has been an excellent place to put my work, it never really does anything. All of us who have our "Readers" are reading the works of others in the choir. We are afraid or too lazy to make the rounds of submitting to reputable publishers, holding off for better, and at least for me, it may be time to move on.

I have started participating in a writer's workshop, where I get all the feedback I care to get, and the others who share their work speak of the heights of the kind of work I tend to read, which is the most crucial point. I still buy books at the local bookstore. We still have them in Berkeley, where I bought the last one. Since someone stole my car, however, I have been inclined not to carry Schmidt's hardcover of *The Story of the Novel*, over 1000 pages, in my backpack slung over my shoulder while I am on the racing bike climbing mountains to work. A Nook never sounded better since it takes an hour to get to work by road and public transport; besides, I am a sweaty mess when I get there. If I were lugging the book around, I would be even sweatier.

I don't read WordPress, but Flavorwire, on occasion, might be the case for the rest of you. Sure, we place our likes like presumptuous pats on the back of our fellow writers, but how often do we read all the way through? Thank God people tend to write only a little or in serial because who has the time?

Again, I spend my time on books I have purchased. I go to a cafe and sit. I do not bring my computer.

Anyway, I am about done: 3,552 views and 194 comments later.

RED POPPIES

November 13, 2014
For the lost soldiers,
Red poppies grace the land.
A sea of them a-butt a castle.
Although they serve one family,
Claiming to be royal,
They are individualized,
Porcelain, almost permanent,
Registered and swaying.
It is a solemn occasion,
How growth comes back.
Once a man, now a poppy,
A useless flower,
Except for its beauty,
Just like any other,
None of which are real.

VIRGINS IN AN ORCHESTRA

December 1, 2015
Plucking, like Chinese virgins in an orchestra.
Angry witch with pasty skin.
The movement of España.
Each shape of the instruments
Represent the bodies of women.
Almost an atonal orchestra.
For some reason, I see dogs in the streets
Tired and hungry and
A woman is singing to them.
Why aren't the animals invited?
Such orchestration.
Everything is so refined.
Two people move in space.
I am dancing invisibly.

SINGLE DOVES

<u>*December 1, 2015*</u>
Rhubarb pressings
Single doves
The fingerings of an undamped massage.
He moves his arms in a white T-shirt.
Wearing gloves,
He taps on metal
Shaped to reflect the sun—it moves in and out
To punch up the tempo.
Aching bass moans quietly—Red, white, and blue.
The bow moves back and forth,
Like single threads to a pattern.

GHOSTS IN HER VOICE

December 1, 2015
There are ghosts in her voice,
The flutter of energy passes through her vocal cords.
One night, three voices
Flow through the spaces of our minds and ears.
Singing to each other
Under white light.
In unison.
The poet reads,
Trying to catch up.
You can barely hear him,
But his words carry weight and tears,
Narration for the ghost,
The whining banshees of Fado.

NO RAINY-DAY FRIEND

February 29, 2016
The morning wakes.
It is the first light.
Tied to a trunk,
I am like the
The rampart of a colossal ship
The fabric is from the sail
Of a boat from Trinidad
The twine taken from the cleats
I set the clothes to dry.
By morning,
I hear the seashore,
Which put me to bed.
I dream of the ocean.
I swing in the wind.
I go over all the lovers I have had
Down the list of bodies and
Faces.
We went to places together,

Became intimate for moral reasons.
I ended up here.
Tied to a pole,
Somewhat comfortable with the beauty of the idea,
But not so much with the warmth.
Because, as a man, I have let no one in.
I chose my freedom
Tethered to a tree
As far away from others
I have shared and then forgotten
Until they come to me like ghosts
That makes up the landscape of myself.
You may come to me and
Knock at the invisible door,
But I am just like the weather vane,
No rainy day friend.

THE DEFINITION OF HOPE

February 29, 2016
The incremental simplicity of desire
A single string between his
Happiness and our hearing
He plays the guitar as if it is his last hope.
He puts everything into it.
What we never offered to teach,
He introduced himself.
With nothing except a momentary good fortune,
We were able to see.
The artist depends on the willingness of strangers.
He believes in a God that will take care of him.
But, if we all have single-string guitars
and await our chances,
Who will come to our need?

COINCIDENCE

May 10, 2016

You sit for a second on the bench, and then the view is gone. It's some room fit with equipment and a bathroom. The breezes blow across your face, and then there is darkness, and the "I" disappears. Every second is a gift: every thought, a timely prayer. No matter how it differs from television or the movies, every relationship is real. I think we are always withholding love. We don't recognize the people we are with, in every aspect, in each moment, but they are the US. We are all the same, in the same thoughts, looking out eyes that cannot see ourselves, only each other, and we still don't recognize it. We are of one mind. On the level of the "I," we are the same. We can learn to love if we practice taking risks with strangers. I believe in coincidence.

YESTERDAY, I SMELLED A DEAD MAN'S BODY

May 14, 2016
Yesterday, I smelled a dead man's body.
And the flies knew before I did,
Like some new restaurants, they were
At the door, even going underneath.
I repeatedly knocked, and no one answered.
One minute standing and the next
Unconscious forever.
I saw the man, thin, goateed, gray-haired
Seemingly viable, kind, and soft-spoken.
His car was without hubcaps; one of those
Light Toyotas, dark-colored like the night sky.
He always wore the same jacket, pants, and shirt
That matched his car.
We had cordial conversations and only a little more.
I never thought to bother him.
We have our own lives.

Maybe he lost his job,
Fell off a ladder,
I had a heart attack;
I don't know.
There was a gentleman's silence.
Between us.
No family, no wife, no children,
Perhaps the economy is to blame:
Enron, Bank of America, anything
Too big to fail?

DOORBELLS ON THE LAWN

<u>*June 7, 2016*</u>
It is missing in light
Growing
Refractions of you
Adding in subtraction
Loss and envy
Evergreen complacency and
Doorbells on the lawn.
A guitar strums,
A key is unlocked, and
Two voices blow in the breeze
Inspired.

CUP HOLDER

June 23, 2016

I was at my mother's skilled nursing facility and wondered why they would put these cup holders in the grass. You could lie down and enjoy a drink without spilling, except that the close-cropped grass wouldn't cause a spill anyway and that it was, after all, astroturf, and it was outside. I also thought rather insensitively that some patients might only lie down, and there was a cup holder. They were far apart so that you wouldn't have people lying on each other. My, how thoughtful these places are.

WHEN YOU BREAK UP

June 28, 2016

"I forgot our anniversary," the man said to his visibly angered wife, "because I am busy." He left the dinner table at the restaurant and walked off. They had been bickering, and he got up to go and said goodbye after paying the check and dropping his napkin. She was on the phone for a while with someone else. She eventually left. The whole room could tell they were fighting.

He wrote to a woman he had quickly made love to yesterday. On the first date, she asked him, "Do you want to make love now or later?"

He told her to be perceived as a gentleman, he would wait. They waited a few days.

By the third date, she had an emotional breakdown in a Left Bank restaurant. After two nights at her house, she was exhausted from travel. The day before, she went to see her step-sister, whom she seldom saw, and her father, who was recovering from cancer, caused tears to come down her face. She had driven from Santa Cruz to Marin and back to Menlo

Park. She was hungry. She had massaged an older man, who fell asleep in her arms but mostly wanted to sing.

Her meltdown, the irrational behavior that came before it, and his inability to relate since he had not gone through those feelings with her left him empty. He told her about another occurrence that he could not connect to his friend's mother's death because he had lost his father when he was ten.

"Good for the bastard," he said, "maybe it would treat him to be less of a bully."

But, of course, that was the worst thing he could have said. He even asked and got to see her mother.

In the meantime, almost the point of this, he thought, was that she sang and played the guitar for him and used his poems/words from his books to write songs, leading him to draft a collaborative contract if she wanted to do an album.

That is the point, he said. Even though she told him he was terrific, she probably couldn't trust or feel it was worth it. All she wanted was to keep her distance. He demonstrated a lack of empathy. The point, he thought, was how and why you don't sleep with the people you work with because things get complicated. A line crossed, and everything seemed to say, "No. I would rather not." Things come out of nowhere, and all you want to do is stay away.

That's what happens when you break up. You say to yourself, "It is just not worth it."

SON OF A HOARDER

September 28, 2016

On Lewers Street in Waikiki, a hotel was halfway down the street, between Kalia Street and Kalakaua Blvd, where he lived with his mother. The mouth of the road that fed the Sheraton Waikiki on the Makaha (North) side came out in front of the hotel, 260 Annex. It mainly housed residents. A woman dying of leukemia was in one of the units down the hall.

On the ground floor was a Chinese restaurant called House of Hong. Tourists would enter the Chinese-style red-painted wood entrance to the restaurant. As a local, he would marvel at the implied wealth of men and women in business attire and laughter. In the cinder block wall hallway was a plain blue carpet. He looked down at it and imagined how thick the padding must have been. The humidity and the temperature were the same as it was outside. The owners never air-conditioned the hallways, which led to stairwells on either end of the building. The cement stairwells were enclosed with glass windows, always open. You could see between the hotels and down into the narrow driveways. As he looked from the

8th floor, it made him queasy. Cars would either go up one floor from the ground level or into the basement. He looked at how dirty the walls were; he knew cars caused black lines and gashes because they could not negotiate the narrow lane.

Sometimes, it rained, but usually only once a day. It would shower as close as across the street, get things wet, then dry out almost immediately. He walked into the rain or waited until it cleared in the hallway fronting the street. It depended on what side of the road you were on and if you wanted to get wet. He would look into the knick-knack store in the hallway to his right as he looked out into the street. The walls were a medium gloss white, glass, or ornate near the House of Hong. He would look into the restaurant at the bar, but he never ate there in all the years he had lived in Hawaii. There was a three-balcony apartment in the last flat on the top floor facing the beach, his mother's place. The carpet was plain and blue, too. He looked down and thought no one had cleaned it. The walls were white and felt thick, unshakable, and solid cement. He never feared that they would fall. He hit them with his hand, and it hurt. He stood inside the threshold and shut the door. He felt embarrassed.

A black and white picture of him in a gray suit was on the inside wall. He thought about his recent divorce. His pants were down in the image, and he held a framed photograph of his ex-wife's portrait, which he had taken. He liked plays within plays. His ex-wife wore a hat with a fabric strap at the bottom of the crown. He looked at her and thought about how much he loved her. She was a pretty Asian woman from Nicaragua; he knew those eyes. She was smiling. He took the picture in almost the same place he hung it. He framed it in red with a turquoise matte and black inner core. He had told his friend Jeff Fleischmann, a framer, what colors and types of materials he wanted. He turned to his right, passing the bathroom door. As soon as he took a shower, he was sweating again. His clothes seemed wet because of the heat and humidity. Everything inside was white or glass.

The bathroom components were as old as the day of installation. He turned toward his bedroom, the only one in the small suite. He realized that his mother had sacrificed for him to be in the room, but she needed him too, but he didn't know how much she needed him. The thought of this would haunt him for the rest of his life. His uncle and aunt had lived in the suite long before his mother. He could sense that she was acting weird with all the trash and accumulation of things. He shared it with her since his divorce. She wouldn't let him throw anything away, and he pleaded with her. After the divorce, he moved into various shared situations, but his roommates made it nearly impossible in every case. He remembered the bassist for the Honolulu Symphony, who was bipolar. The negative energy from this man affected him with oppressive rants. The power was communicable. He couldn't take it.

He installed a lemon-yellow carpet and painted the walls turquoise. He had always wanted to paint his walls another color than white. He vertically put semi-transparent corrugated light green roof panels to give him privacy from the hotel across the street. He was curious to know if the tourists across the way could see him at night. He worried about being seen naked.

He seldom went onto his balcony, in effect, closing himself

off. He wasn't happy about it, but he wanted the look of the material. He suffered the scent of fiberglass and the stagnancy of the air due to the blocked windows. In the balcony next to his, facing Lewers Street, his mother stored several decrepit corrugated boxes containing baskets she had made, plastic-covered natural fiber supported by stiff wood. He remembered her making them when he was a kid. The baskets had fabric interiors and lights on the outside connected to a flashlight inside that provided electricity. He would switch the lights on and off. The last time he checked the boxes, they housed various generations of pigeons and cockroaches, from translucent or opaque eggs to death. He remembered his stepfather loading a truck with his mother's belongings. His mother married, moved twice to the continental US for no longer than a year, and then moved back because her marriages or relationships would end because of the extrarelational affairs of her boyfriends or husbands. Or because of alcohol and abuse. He had trimmed all the plants in the planters near the front door to reflect a Japanese garden, which pissed off his stepfather, for example. His stepfather fought against the Japanese in WWII.

Inside his room was a red plywood desk that he had cut in an organic shape and nailed into a tree stump that looked like a woman's torso turned upside-down. He liked how closely it resembled female anatomy. A long glass stalactite reached the floor and attached to the other end of the table. It was supposed to represent sperm. The table came from his one-person photography show at the University of Hawaii at Manoa that incorporated the desk and a chair made of a black-painted metal rod in an Emmanuelle Chair, like a giant fan.

It wasn't comfortable to sit on, although he cut out a piece of wood that served as a seat. On the desk was the same manual typewriter he had in the show, and on the turquoise walls was a black-and-white picture of a man in drag. He framed the image he got from a colleague, who would later print images in Manhattan for such greats as Andres Serrano, who did 'Piss Christ.' There were foam-core, life-size cutouts of people in various poses with outstretched arms and arched backs. He leaned them against the walls.

He stood for a moment before going into his room. It was hot in the room, and the colors vibrated with tension. He looked at the wooden lattice that blocked his gaze into his mother's area, the 'living room' of the small suite. Fabric covered the lattice, so he couldn't see but knew what was on the other side—a white Vienna-style vinyl sofa with paneled arms that she had reupholstered. Previously, a soft, satiny, wool, paisley-patterned, white-on-white fabric covered it. There was a white, early American table with an inlaid, mother-of-pearl top. He would hit his shins against it in an open room. He knew too of white vinyl chairs somewhere hidden in a mess.

His mother's bed was just inside to the right, in front of the closet filled with her clothes. The room had many Visitor magazine sheets with Sharpies and ball-point pen jottings. This habit would follow her for the rest of her life as she kept notes on advertisements and other printed matter. Two small jagged trails went through the knee-deep clutter to each of the balconies, piled high with cardboard boxes. He imagined what people thought of them as they could see them from balconies in hotel rooms in front and to the right. These were filled with belongings and covered with various blankets. The blankets would shift and expose the newspapers and different household things with a breeze. Her life felt on hold.

She would smoke on the balcony in a corner covered with rope, faux ivy, plastic flowers, a fake parrot, a large ashtray, and a white rod-iron ice cream chair. Those chairs he remembered were always in the family, painted in many colors: white, yellow, black, and pink. She smoked her cigarettes and looked toward the ocean, which you could make out through a break between the Cinerama Reef and Halekulani Hotel. It wasn't far, about half a block, and he would take his surfboard and paddle out to "Threes" or "Popular's" mostly.

The kitchen in the suite was about seven feet long and three feet wide. It was small and dirty. Cabinets above and below the countertops housed a small stove and oven. There were four stove elements. The kitchen felt cramped. To the left was a small sink. There were herds of cockroaches either walking around the floors and counters or hidden. At night, when he turned on the light, they would scurry. They even entered the refrigerator and walked around at times because it was never cold enough to deter them, and the seams were old and uneven, which sickened him and would be one of the reasons he left Hawaii. His mother kept hamburger meat that she ate raw and put in the refrigerator exposed; she couldn't afford plastic wrap. He always disliked this. There were always open containers containing previous meals covered in pamphlets or card stock papers she would collect from the visitor shelves in the various hotel lobbies. He remembered them as brochures about tourist destinations or tours. She used them as stationary.

THE SLOW SAUCE
OF WOOD

October 20, 2016
If the tree could only hear itself
The heart-racing through the years
Each line has four complete seasons
As snow fell and rain danced
As creatures passed and the wind blew
How water moved through its veins
And the light in the morning and
Nightfall caused
A squeeze of fibers
Every circle tells a story
Like awkward rock
Erosion and fluctuations in time
Speak of what confrontations it greeted
How the slow sauce of wood grew year after year.

THE MASK

November 2, 2016

A cell phone lay on a large wooden table surrounded by chairs. Stapled sheets of paper and compiled documents are on the table with a person's name, date, class, and assignment in the upper left-hand corner - each on its line, the title of the work centered on the page, two spaces below, and then two slots below the indented paragraphs that covered the rest of the pages. Several academic papers are on the table in the center of the room on the chair to the right. An open laptop sat on the table. There were glasses, brown-rimmed, probably plastic. Next to those was a light-green dinosaur on a small stack of books and magazines next to the mirrors, a black and orange floral bag, a tall stainless steel mug, and a windbreaker.

Also, on the table lay a black leather purse with gold rhinestones. They ran from the top to the bottom at a diagonal, then around the base and up on the front and back of the purse. There were ball-shaped attachments, diamond-shaped round holes, smaller appliqués, a black strap, and a tan interior. The purse leaned. The bag was new, open, and unblemished. Inside the purse was a strand of aluminum, blue on one side and bright silver on the other. It hit the light just so. There were more strands, then a white rubber mask covered in black shadows near the mouth. Along the hairline of the mask were red beads with strands of white hair moving out through the beads. These beads and hair were all over the head. The eye holes were just big enough so that someone's eyes could see out. The mask crumpled onto itself, and there were crimson splatters.

BOLINAS

December 1, 2016

Today, while on HWY 1 on the way to Bolinas, just before Stinson, I was coming around a sharp corner, and there was a man in a bright red robe and leather boots, the hood of the robe over his head, and backpacks on his back. He stuck out his thumb, and I stopped. He said he was going to the North Pole to help Santa. He called me Sir; it seemed like he was in his twenties. His cheeks were full. I drove him to Bolinas, and we went our separate ways.

HERDING COWS

<u>*January 4, 2017*</u>
Money drives the cows in this land.
A treacherous sea of willing souls
Aimless and perfunctory.
Frightened by the mill
That churns their bodies,
They have no other movement
But forward.
It is not a movement we would recognize:
To carry arms and play army.
But most men
Have no purpose in America,
Don't measure their actions,
Don't take into account what they are doing.
From Mexico to Oregon,
The grass-fed cows walked.
Their loins lean, and their
Flesh gamey.
What was weird was
That the fat they had was orange
And twisted.

It coated the system with
A plaque that only angioplasty
Could be removed.
The doctor, if they made it that far,
Would take a simple wire
With a sharp tip and bang the insides
Of the aorta, and all the plaque would
Be absorbed by the body.
Their hearts were still at risk;
Once you dislodged the truth,
It would migrate
To the brain and cause a stroke.

WRITING TO STRANGERS

<u>*January 8, 2017*</u>

You are a tiny bit taller; could you shave your calluses, and I could grow a head of hair? I like that you are kind. You'll have to be; my intelligence is all I have. I am optimistic about literature and art and indulge myself in reading. I wrote a story today. I take that back. I published a report that I wrote long ago on my blog. It is incredible how closely we adhere to a type of writing and look at things differently. I was married; it was raining. The island of Oahu flooded. It was New Year's.

I read a piece that said that lasting relationships need only a bit of kindness. I think you've hit that nail on the head. Tenderness and charm are fun to look at and feel, as with being cared for and garnering affection, you say there's this passion and wildness.

I believe in the truth. That's basically how a person feels. As I get older, who attracts me becomes less and less tempted. I am at the stage where I have to pretend I am not interested because if interest is made known, there might be laughter if I am lucky. Often, it is discomfort and, at times, anger. The word "creepiness" comes up. As a Cancer, you might understand the absolute truth in this. As a Cancer, I know it and obey it, too.

I am very romantic. I have to be in love to make love. Otherwise, I would rather be alone. But, like you, I am tired. I read something recently saying there are no second thoughts with love. So they often tell me I can settle; there are parts of people I can live with, but usually not the whole, so I do not pay attention. The last woman I was in love with was in '99. The rest have been measured against and failed. There are so many details to deal with that the task seems impossible. In a cameo in the movie *The Sheltering Sky*, Bowles said that we only fall in love 4 to 5 times, then die. I have fallen in love three times, and they were my opposite. Of late, a woman wrote stories antithetical to my own. I tend to write about unrequited love. I reach out only to have my hand slapped.

I have written and made art so many times that I am at this phase where I am only saving my money to retire. At times, I get tired of reading. Caitlin Moran's *How to Be a Woman* tells me who you might be. Next is Siri Hustvedt's *A Woman Looking At Men Looking At Women*. I wrote a book that forgets some of this title. In Moran's treatise, I see that women have the same drives; our bodies are victims of chemistry and visual stimulus. I love Moran's language. Her English phrases are halting and fun. I like how the English leave out definite articles and say "university" or "hospital," for example.

I want to wake up next to some fleshy force that gets me giddy and racing. I want to hear lovely-expressed words that make me sweat and writhe. I don't want to wake up alone. I need devotion and blind love. I like the grit of life.

TRIBU CAFE

January 10, 2017

An assortment of fern and other green plants in tin and metal planters move erratically in the wind. The metal gate signifies a boundary, perhaps on sunnier days when one could imagine tables and chairs with white tablecloths aflutter in late spring and October.

The structure that houses the Tribu Cafe is modern, with its thick cement walls and square pillars. The melody of bass and piano lightly fills my heart with the mellow magic of love. Two people (bassist and pianist) not even looking at each other meld spiritually.

It makes me think of my life and where I can go next. It colors the bland LOW-COST APPLIANCES – SALES – SERVICE sign across the street.

Izumi stands at a distance listening and then comes over: "Writing a book?" she says.

"No, this experience," I say.

When listening to music, words, phrases, sentences, paragraphs, and stories get shortened. Every human being takes on a glow. The women become more beautiful, and the men become friends.

I can't help but notice a woman who looks like Kristen Stewart, her thin presence. Her controlling activities, her man, are sitting around the corner, out of sight.

I'm going through a period where I recognize that those I am attracted to are no longer attracted to me and vice versa. I also sense that the next phase of life will be about substance and conversation and less about sex. I will be learning about women.

Nao looks up in the air as she plays the piano. The bassist, Mark Williams, plays beautifully. What does that mean, I imagine? It is a bit of voice whispering eloquent phrases like T.S. Eliot's poetic works, pulsations of the heart. "While he took from them their ability to infuse poetry with high intellectualism while maintaining a sensuousness of language."

"Rainy Day jazz lunch," Izumi says.

Across the street, a young man kisses his girl at the light. She seems delighted. He looks down at his cell phone; she carries a pizza box. Her delight fades to purposefulness. His, however, is like that of a happy journalist. That journalist hears juicy news and then shares it with the world. She must have seen or felt me, all seriousness after that. I'm like an assessing presence, a killjoy, a troll.

Meanwhile, Izumi sings: "Our love is here to stay?"

"What are you thinking? What are you going through?" She continues. Cars pass. People have destinations, responsibilities, and places where they want to be. The thought of the president-elect consumes our time. We don't see ourselves against the backdrop. How fragmented is our purpose? Our roles? How do we fit? The melody softens our self-criticism and loves us as we are.

Izumi sings. Nao will eventually go back to Japan. I am alone on the side of the room with sunshine, but everyone has left—shadowed by the other side, empty seats. Izumi is courteous and looks over at me, singing to the room as a whole: "My heart serenading you... My prelude to a kiss."

Caitlin Moran says her sexual interests arose with puberty in *How to Be a Woman*. Chemical and physical properties at work make this music internally-reaching.

A dog jumps into a car with a mere suggestion of its female owner, a man at the wheel. She gets in, has a minimal conversation, and they drive away.

Often, this is the essence of life: familiarity and experience. The rain has stopped.

Another couple is on the phone in purple running shoes, and she adjusts her shoe and looks back.

This other woman, Kristen Stewart, also looks like Lauren Bacall. I've become suspicious of her.

I think the instrumental leaves an open space for my voice to fit, but then Izumi's singing also conjures the desire to sing along.

"I can give you anything but love.

Lauren Bacall and her man are outside laughing. The laughter feels meant for me, but I am sure oblivious to them.

For example, I do not have relationships built on time spent maneuvering among and between personalities. I close my eyes, expecting to see someone I know, and turn away to see if they'll sit beside me. But I am delusional, such as not learning about the long line of suitors other than me. We, men, pay no attention to other men, busy with the women on whom we have crushes.

Rain shadows the mountains in the background. The girl with her dog passes.

A woman with her boyfriend sits at my table late for the event. She sings to her boyfriend: "Why Not Take All Of Me?" Her voice is lovely. I wanted to ask Izumi to have the band back her, but they played the last song. I say this because in the back of my mind is this poem Emily Rosen wrote that explains the unification of women's and men's desire to be acknowledged for the greatness and talent they feel they have. At the moment, the couple sitting next to me has reduced the conversation. The food arrives. They eat, and she coughs toward me. She sipped and began singing louder: "Why not take all of me?" She reaches toward me and takes the salt shaker with a vengeance. She wants to be recognized and allowed to be a part of the room's focus, which is now the bassist and the friends of Izumi (all women) in various states of departure.

This late arrival keeps singing while the Raiders game is on. There's quiet in the room. The late arrival wants to be part of the melody of life, be found in our individuality, have something to give, and be of value, which becomes apparent.

The couple talks about having given time without compensation. Someone got the man's music lessons for free. We offer our souls for free. I have argued for an economy based on men's and women's purposes, but we would all sit around humming to each other and live in places like the Ghost Ship, drinking coffee.

THE TRUTH

January 25, 2017

You either employ the truth and uphold it, or you deny it. The truth is always there. It seems to implicate a decision, whereas making that decision seems to go against our better judgment when we can't see a way out. It sometimes goes against what appears to be for the better, at least on the surface. Going with the truth seems to imply some faithful leap, but often, we are forced to go to the edge and jump. There is no way to avoid it. It is old and willing to wait; it is your only relationship with time: eternity. You are afraid of pushing yourself into what you know you must do. To be good is what your spirit desires. The whisper is constant; we make beautiful things with ourselves and others. We have beautiful insides. We love and care. We have this empathy for others. We are often overwhelmed with what we are supposed to do. But that is all that life is, this constant giving and believing. The head fights the heart; everything we do sometimes is against logic. But the heart is courageous, not cold, not unkind. Good lives inside. Bad dies.

FIRST LOVE POEM

March 13, 2017
Sophia sips coffee
In Oakland, irreverently.
She pushes paper while listening.
Knitting a hammock to lie in,
There's dog-walking and
Yoga, cooking, and Coptic bookbinding
As explained in The Private Library.
She's closed the chapter on the end of the world.
She says it's her word against time.
She bakes her way into silver linings
Via two-steps.
She hears the Withering Spoon.
Reality is fictionalized through
Witchery and Wild Love.
Sources her ethics
Through Americans, pillows, and breakfast.
Her mouth is an art object.
Hiking with puppies
And I was binging on Netflix.
I am curious

Want to share, and
Grow together like hair.
I ride my bike to get Euphoria.
Could this be you?
I like ice cream, but my body
Loathes it.
I have photography at the Oakland Museum,
But it is locked away.
I would love to make more.
With you, and I don't mind dirt.
I love hiking and conversations,
But not steep overlooks.

AS A WRITER

<u>October 13, 2017</u>

As a writer who typically or should stay home to write and read without distraction but does so to be among the living, I love this place, where they also have salads. They may have a branch in WC, where I have heard music and poetry readings.

What if you were sitting there and I thought you were interesting? You seem substantial and intelligent. How else would I get to know you? How would we meet? Don't we need such a neutral zone for our first date? Anyway, I am intrigued by this. I would love to see where you have your coffee and what kind you like.

As my title says, I am a cafe writer. Are you giving me a chance to redeem myself by responding to me?

I see the word "sarcasm" in your repertoire. I always wonder about this in psychological terms. Inherently, it means to insult. All the pretty girls in grade school dating other boys used it. It stems from intelligence and confidence. They were that. My father died when I was 10; I was sarcastic before that. So, when a woman is sarcastic with me, it triggers a kind of sadness in memory of a free and easy time. I got everything I wanted. My father was a successful urologist, and my mother was a commercial artist and fashion model.

She "smoked regularly," which seems not to bother her. She remains in a nursing home with Alzheimer's.

I would love to know your artistic side, the painting.

I have never read *The Greenage Summer*. The title seems intriguing. When was the green age?

I either read or watched *The Scarlet Letter*. Wasn't it with a brunette actress as the woman who wanted to chat with him? I can't remember her name, but the storyline seems to follow less hopefully than *The Notebook*, which is not genuinely hopeful either. The heart follows no rules but does feel them.

Twin Peaks and all of Lynch's movies are significant to me as an artist. He makes me think about the importance of culture and the complexity of life.

I want to listen to Sublime with you.

I am reading William Gass's book *On Being Blue* about your favorite color. I bought it because I opened it, and the first words I read were: "What a page before was a woman suddenly a breast, and then a nipple, then a little ring of risen flesh, a pacifier, water bottle, rubber cushion. Without plan or purpose, we slide from substance to sensation, a fact to feel, all outcomes in, and we hear only exclamations of suspicious satisfaction: the mums, the ohs, the aha" p. 17. He is talking about how sex has to be about something else because to speak of it precisely diminishes what is arousing. Then he cites Henry Miller, who writes in such a way as to talk about something else entirely, and yet it is all about sex and how we feel and think about it, because, given our puritanical upbringing, that's the only way we can enjoy it. It reminds me of another book by Wilhelm Stekel about fetishism: At war with inner reality, p. 21.

The citation appealed to me because I am working on a piece about how women respond to men.

I have no sense of humor. I am a *Man Without Qualities*, another excellent book by Robert Musil.

Anyway, I go on. How was your cup of coffee?

CHRISTMAS BREAKFAST

<u>*December 28, 2018*</u>

The dining table has no hanging lamp but a track of wire upon which the lights are screwed and electrified. They are little flying saucers in brushed aluminum. My dining room and kitchen combine birch wooden doors, white high-gloss cabinets, and light gray-blue walls.

The whitened window drapes hang a foot from the ceiling to the floor. A top sirloin steak is cooking—the oil snaps. The scent of pepper radiates. I am not supposed to be eating it. I am a heart patient. You should have seen Christmas Breakfast: The Mimosas and the Vanilla Crown Royal, not to mention the biscuits, eggs, gravy, melon, and sausages.

The house breathes. I let the air in through a bedroom window. It's winter, Christmas Day, and I always leave that window open no matter how cold. I still need oxygen at only 11:34 PM, but I am usually up until 4 AM.

I don't do taverns nor drink; bars intimidate me. Our country is only 200 years old. On the West Coast, my condo changes almost every day. I remodeled and painted the molding white. It's the first coat. It sucks, and it wants more. The steak is resting.

I prefer the cinema to a cold drink. I would rather have catharsis than sleepiness. I know you would think that without sex, a man would choose to eat and drink, but I intellectualize. It's been so long without love that I see a woman as just another person—dressed up for her own sake. What interest would she have in me? At this age, what good would I have in her? We are like broken tanks on the battlefield. Neither of us moves. We look across at our bodies, somewhat accepting of the facts. It's over. We've had our campaign. I feel like a criminal for having no feelings for her, and it feels like a crime for those I do have feelings for. Women are jailbait at every age. You feel confined to them, or you seem to abuse them. Money does not break down the wall. I assume it ultimately leaves you defeated. Worthless. After all, any dominant being that takes advantage of another ends up spiritually bankrupt because the world finally deals in the truth, the currency. Ask Donald Trump. How long has he lasted?

Yes, I am resting. I had my steak, which was mostly gristle. The smell still permeates the air. There are specks of grease on my glasses. There are pieces of meat that get between my teeth. I am thinking about dental floss.

I am not obeying anyone, but that will change when I work.

I long for the coffee shop before work. It is winter, as I said. I walked outside in my socks to a friend's, and I could feel the dampness of the cement—the chill. The dog would not go swimming, but she drank the water. The sun was out like she was on a movie set. The light was radiant. Oh, but I said that, didn't I? The sun radiates, as does the pepper.

A "meet-up." I remember those. Every event was a veiled desire to get laid, find love, and live happily ever after. But money and time always get in the way: "So, what do you do for a living?"

"I am a dragonfly; I fly around and eat mosquitos." I can't tell them what I do. I pick up garbage. Who wants to boast about a man who picks up other people's trash? Besides, I smell like garbage. You can't get it out. Like garlic, it sticks with you. I have great, big, brutish arms that women who have met me in passing admire, but I am too hairy. "Chia seeds" cover my body. I look like an ape. I brush a long strand of loose hair back with my glove when I lift the container via the arm of the garbage truck. I realize I contradict my sleeping habits. I wake at 5 AM and head to the facility for my vehicle.

Summer days are sweaty and smelly like sour swill. But I have been on dates that involved strolls along the beach. When we get to that question, everything changes. I get the look of immediate disconnection: that question, that question. I am the Philistine; even though it's obvious, I am not guided by materialism nor disdainful of intellectual or artistic value.

I don't spend much time bathing, although I probably should. I am not feeling the situation nor of stilling pain. I am beyond that. I have two children who live with my divorced wife.

So, yes, we agree. I am on an empty train alone, in continued and deadly enmity.

I imagine park benches, except where I live, there are Black Crowned Night Heron, Great Blue Herons, California

Brown Pelicans as well as White Pelicans, Mallard Ducks, Cormorants, Snowy Egrets, Great Egrets, Cranes, Forester Terns, Canadian Geese, and Coots to name a few. They leave evidence that these city-dwellers aren't necessarily wealthy, and gardens are often rugged. You hear those birds or the passing traffic.

I have no connection to anyone. It's not funny. There are two parts to me: the realist and the optimist. Each piece gets along like roommates in a small apartment, and I must get up by five if I want to get to work on time.

NEW YEAR

<u>*January 4, 2019*</u>

I once applied to stay in a treehouse in Scotland to be alone and do art. I didn't get chosen. I told them I was related to the first king of Scotland. They must have laughed. I didn't mention that I did stand-up or play the piano. I don't say I play the piano because it is the iPhone piano, which is funny. My neighbors are restless. They cannot tell where the music is coming from. I pretend I am alone in the forest; the speakers are on the balcony, above the pool. It's New Year's. My sliding glass door is open. If I could write what it sounds like, I would. Di-ling-ling-ling-ling-ling or something like that.

I sent my music (248 songs) to Michael Tilson Thomas's agent, who lives in London. It cost me $84, not including the flash drive. Who will put a flash drive from a stranger on their computer? I also sent a flash drive to the Director of the Sacramento Symphony. I did that because my mother took me to the symphony as an extremely young child. You wonder about that kind of child when you are in a fancy restaurant. "When will this child start screaming?" Well, I didn't scream. I was stupefied. Red velvet, my mother, the runway model, descendent of Mary McCall, apparently a cousin of Robert the Bruce, but you'd never know. The lineage is on a website with a black background. Have you ever read a webpage with a black background? The white font, which blinds you, is like seven. So forget that. At this rate, I can't tell the Kinlosses from the Kincardines; besides, I do laundry and don't even have the heat on in the apartment.

I applied to stay in the woods and make art. It didn't happen, or why else would I be here telling you? Instead, I picked up the piano (the iPhone, which has a piano) and played during lunch in a restaurant. Believe it or not, the restaurant was called "Small Wonder" during lunch, and they were paying me with food and drink, which I never asked for, except once, because frankly, I couldn't believe it. Was I getting paid for playing music in a restaurant? How does that happen? I went from making phone calls and knowing nothing about music to playing stuff that actually "sounds good" to a music teacher but "has no melodies," he said, which, of course, is silly. I looked up "melody," and it says: "A sweet or agreeable succession or arrangement of sounds," which to me seems to define "Sounds nice," but what do I know?

OK, let's get down to what happened tonight. I was coming home from my sister's; we had Chinese food. It's New Year's. We talked about my mother. God Rest Her Soul. She was a hoarder with Alzheimer's, and I couldn't save her because it would have meant I stopped living for myself. After all, my mother needed that much time. I remember being worried if my mother got enough food, which she must have since she lived in an independent living arrangement where they fed her three meals daily. Still, for some reason, when I saw her refrigerator, it contained various exposed foods, even hamburger, which I knew she took from the package, applied salt and pepper, and ate. She did that when we lived in Honolulu in a hotel where roaches ran around, and the refrigerator wasn't cold nor wholly sealed.

We talked about my mother, and my sister said, as she always does, that our mother was OK. But I am deeply saddened to know that she never continued with what she started being: a runway model and a commercial artist.

While driving back, I saw a man with a blanket wrapped around his head pushing himself down the sidewalk. It was 33ºF degrees. I went past him and thought: "I am not going to let a man in a wheelchair freeze to death," so I circled back, parked next to him, and asked him through the open window: "Do you need anything?" And he said, "Yes, I could use some water."

I told him to meet me at the gas station, up the street where he seemed to be heading, and I would get it for him. He never made it that far. I gave him the water and asked him if he needed anything: "How about a warm jacket?"

He replied, "Well, yes. I could use that. I've got this old one on," which I overlooked since the blanket covered him.

"How about a sleeping bag?" I added.

He said, "Sure!"

"OK," I gave him the water and said: "I will get those for you and meet you here."

It took me a while, but I went to Target and bought him a down jacket, a lovely faux fur hat to cover his ears, thick gloves, socks, sandwiches, juices, fruit, and the sleeping bag, ranked 25ºF. I hooked those things onto the back of his wheelchair. He had been going up a slight hill, pushing himself, facing backward, when I found him near the intersection across the street from the train the second time. One shoe was nearly off. He smelled. I tucked his blanket down his back because it got caught in the wheel. He thanked me and seemed excited. I didn't know what else to do.

None of this was funny. I wasn't alone in the woods. I didn't joke about playing the piano and getting paid for food and drink. I had a house and complained about work. The heater is on; I am remodeling my condo. Can you imagine being him? Can you imagine being even yourself or me? What are we doing with our lives? I read yesterday that Heidegger said Caring is the fundamental disposition of Da-Sein, which is Being-in-the-world.

I wanted to talk about The New Year in terms of Heidegger. He said, "What always is is what is constantly here." Happy New Year!

THE PARADE

April 1, 2019

I met a man in a bar. He told me to come to meet Dr. Rudy.

I met Dr. Rudy again, and he remembered me.

Simon suggested I write him a letter. "A little step at a time. Make an appointment. Ask him if he can take a little time to hear one piece, and then ask him to suggest the next step."

Then, I went to the lake.

I played, staring across the water at a woman.

No-one stopped.

They did smile. Everyone smiles at a man with a toy piano.

A man with a cane, one arm pulled in close, the leg on that side of his body dragged along for the ride. He wiped his nose with a hand that seemed more accessible and somewhat coordinated with his impulses. He stood halfway to the counter, then approached it like a body ready for a doctor.

The older woman with a thick textbook ordered fruit and granola. She wore a hound's tooth overcoat, a black dress with black nylons, black heels, and a black pouch. She picked at her skin while reading. Her head moved from side to side as if she were shivering. It was hot and sunny outside. It was Sunday. To whom did she interview? What was she studying?

I sense the end myself. The body parades all its grief eventually.

ASHES TO ASHES

<u>*Aug. 27, 2019*</u>

(Ashes to Ashes - The dating app for the rest of us is brought to you by Hasbeen and Associates).

Dating apps have yet to work for me. Whether by my declared age or what measure, it led me to failure.

But it made sense to me when I figured I was swiping based on whether or not I would want to sleep with the woman whose picture I was viewing.

If they were too young or attractive, I am sure they scrutinized me against many more youthful and handsome men.

Even when chosen, I doubted their sincerity or motive, usually correctly, and either didn't know what to say or didn't want to say anything.

Online dating reinforces our stereotypes about who will make a good mate, sex partner, or whatever our motivations were for choosing the app.

Those most appealing visually for both genders were swiped right. Perhaps they were the only ones who swiped right; the rest of us floundered on the sidelines.

Tinder is like going to a party and seeing the most attractive woman. Everyone wants her. As the party wears on and everyone has made eye contact or dared to get rejected and struck out, they move to other possibilities.

But, given so little data, there is a limit to making another decision.

People get bored with rejection and leave the party altogether.

Some bodies were getting lucky.

It wasn't mine.

I am certainly not willing to pay for rejection.

No algorithm will override my inherent bias in picking who would not choose me in the first place.

Almost everyone who chose me was not my "type." It's hard facing facts.

Instead, I would remain delusional and quiet rather than face more truth about my outlying chances.

I am looking for *After Burn, Ashes, Dust to Dust,* or other sites.

Lucky for me and the rest unlucky on those dating apps, *Dust to Dust* is a new app that humps *Tinder* for cast-offs. Like Edward T. Hall's famous scientific anecdote about rats in a cardboard box, all secondary and tertiary rats waiting for the drunk and rejected will get a chance.

The algorithm for *Dust to Dust* surveys all the left-swiped individuals and invites them to a social; after that entry, all participants sign waivers and then shoot up with an anti-inhibitor.

They are led into a dark room via a single-file corridor with rave-type music and asked to remove their clothes, lubricated with vanilla oil, and then pushed into the crowd.

I just remembered that everyone is blindfolded.

You can imagine how feeling lucky turns into feeling scared, and dating or hooking up seems like the last thing you want.

People are always picky about whom and how they have sex.

Those who eventually make it out of the "party" through the trap doors or behind the scenes, given sympathetic employees, have provided the app with no stars and eye-curdling descriptions of events.

Many of us were less than hopeful at the outset:

Mate selection is alive and well.

We are *toast* in a dinner and dancing world.

Did I mention movies? I don't know about you, but I will be going alone.

SONG FOR CORONA

April 23, 2020
I wake you on the dance floor.
The shifting moods of time.
In this limelight, the amber horns of honesty
Permeate the room.
Nevermore shall I encase these dreams.
On top of this is sorrow.
Everyone I loved is gone.
All the memories have failed.
Even in song, the sorrows blossom.
The mixture of my anguish and sweetness
Charms the silence, too.
The squirrels tumble.
The sun is humbled.
Bushes in the garden have their thorns.
A crown has been placed on your head.
You don't wear it well.
By nightfall, I sleep again.
I don't like grief or pain;

I know they are the same.
I need more words for life.
I hover on just a few.
The sorrows that spell my
Life are hand-me-downs.
Trouble is a friend,
And so is silence.
Never doubt the truth that comes to you.
Nothing makes sense, but it will.
This time is full of ghosts, who were surprised.
We were naked at the outset,
Told to say our goodbyes:
"Once I intubate you, you may not wake."
So much of this is science fiction.
So much of this is fate.
I stumble forward,
Stumble out of bed.
They laid me on my stomach and
Paralyzed my legs.
You have my mind in swirling overtures.
The groundwork you must do.
From dust to dust, we swing.
Two partners in a marathon.
Two friends in different countries are
Playing other songs.
Our wrecks group them.
The tumbling notes compartmentalize our eyes.
I see by not questioning the gait.
The fake bunny runs ahead,
Like a funeral march that repeats.

Or a school song played to the parents
Whose children are dead?
I take my gun to the closet.
It's a scam.
They knock on the door or call me.
They want my information.
Our numbers are up.
No, take a number.
You will be called.
Take a number, and she'll never call you.
She's too upset.
I always went for girls whose boyfriends wept.
I am in the market
With falling stock.
The bellicose troubadours are on the sidewalk.
Hair comes out from windows.
As do lots of flies.
There is a marcher.
He is the black shape of today.

YELLOW DRESS

May 25, 2020

Bald, with a shiny head and black glasses, eyebrows tapering at the sides, one eye bigger and the other higher, one ear back and one ear forward; the mouth as one straight line. The shadow of the hair beneath his skin, how the gray cotton sweats, the olive green undershirt, how he sat sternly without a flinch, straight without blinking, military eyes, muscular, but more as an attitude than a build, he pointed his head.

In the satiny yellow dress, your legs crossed on a higher stool than he was, seemingly on a stage, his eyes at the level of your crossed knees. Had you uncrossed them, he might have peered.

You didn't dare uncross them. You pointed your crossed legs as far left as you could get them. Your back ached. Both hands were on your knees. Your head is taut at the neck, pointing at him, but only because you thought staring back would get his respect. But you didn't say a thing about his grip on you.

Judgmental, crossed-over, way too over the line, but there you were. The city was expensive. Just outside and down the street were the strung-out drug dealers and the stains on the concrete, the smell of urine, and a kind of fear that you were almost as close as they were to having nothing to show for yourself but a type of speech that was more drama than truth. You thought of the man with silver hair and a thin jacket lying on the ground versus the man who had built up corrugated boxes and barricaded himself in the doorway.

You thought of this and the transaction at the door of Piano Fight and Red-light Lit. They wrote about sexual innuendo, but here it was real. This guy was paying you. In that thought, you released your legs. Or, at least, the tension gave way. All the muscles in your arms and legs melted.

He watched you. He smiled. His hands went up before his mouth, and he crossed his fingers. Only his eyes looked at you through his glasses that reflected the open laptop screen. His hands dropped quickly; his left hand went up, one finger across one nostril, and the others were in a fist that covered his mouth. His thumb went under his chin and back to his throat. He felt like his hand kept him from moving forward, although he sensed he had won.

You giving in also caused him to soften. It was like a non-verbal concession. You had what he wanted, and he had what you needed because it was all over if you didn't come up with the rent. Where was your next meal? You were alone, except for the certainty. Two people were in a room staring until they agreed.

You uncrossed your legs, and he saw that you weren't wearing anything, and you let him. In fact, for a second, you even went up on your toes and moved your legs as far apart as possible. You felt the edges of your labia part; the air moved in with a breath, and you sat there looking into the furthest corner of the ceiling.

He got out of his chair and walked over. He placed one hand on one leg and the other on the other and pulled your dress back. You were utterly exposed. You looked down at yourself and said: "What was the big deal?"

His head was next to your mouth; he sweated; you smelled him. You closed your eyes, and one tear fell onto your yellow dress.

GRAVITAS

<u>*May 28, 2020*</u>

I watched a parade or a dance troupe in a mall, laid down on two seats, was comfortable, was with friends, and my legs stuck out. It was a faux pas, yes, but I wanted this. To be next to these people, I knew. I lay there as the festivities continued. The sounds went on, and then a person, who I thought was a woman, lay alongside me, thick-armed, soft, and I embraced her holding me. After all, a homeless woman I had known had been curling up inside me earlier and was licking my neck. It was like I accepted her, not finding her smell offensive or her lack of teeth horrifying. I was trying to embrace the problem of man. I inevitably wanted out; I am a germaphobe.

While I was lying there, a woman dressed up for the festivities, a beauty, came over, and while smiling, she questioned the person wrapped around me. Her words told me she was addressing a man: "Johnny (or something this person said), what are you doing?" She tried to pull his arms. She thought we were a couple since I wasn't resisting. She eventually moved on.

At that point, I was very uncomfortable. Why would any man think it was OK to maltreat someone he had never met unless he was gay or thought I was crossing a line as I lay across two chairs and had my feet stick out?

I held steady and remained quiet. I didn't want to test "Johnny." I had to figure out a way so he wouldn't break my neck. Do I grab his balls? Do I put my arms between my neck and his arms? Do I yell for help? At this point, I realized men's passive-aggressiveness and understood what women must feel. Men are the danger. They have no right to pretend to be Gods.

SOMEONE ELSE'S LIFE

<u>*July 3, 2020*</u>

My Iranian friend suggested it would take 20 years for China to take over America, but I surmised we were almost there. The introduction of coronavirus speeds the unfolding. We are in a mad race to zero, from "the greatest nation in the world" to that which will exact the lowest wages and most strenuous work. Many jobs will evaporate.

We thought living in barracks and working 14 hours was wrong, the treatment of screams, like a concentration camp, and people telling on each other to those with the power to flip you off or even shoot you for rebellion.

We thought the lines were long in the depression. In 2020, there will be no lines. Your $11,000 in unemployment will evaporate as fast as you can drink Voilà. If you are lucky, you will have enough money to buy your meals of raw vegetables, put them in an Igloo, and drive to your worksite. You sleep in your car between the four-day, 12-hour increments, then schlep back from your three days off with vegetables for your meals and remain quiet, holed up somewhere.

There is no loyalty. It is only life or death. Sisters will turn on their brothers, and brothers will eye their positions at these factories as their only hope as the assembly lines kick their asses and then kick them to the ground. If they aren't the fastest, most flawless, and most compliant workers, millions are eager to take their jobs, cars, and Igloos full of raw vegetables.

It works like this in movies: single men watching TV in coffin-sized homes stacked in darkness, poorly ventilated fragments, and separated by chicken wire. You had to be close to your jobs. They stole things. Lucky if you had someplace to lay your head, fortunate if you had something coming in. But this upheaval was predictable even without the introduction of COVID-19. We should have known with our leaders not to recommend masks. The intention was to sicken as many as possible and clear the ranks so the government could take social security, pensions, property, and money. Broken lives would surely follow, and everyone in shock clamored not to save the country, as it was, but themselves, for they could see what was happening before the first outsourced human.

The sweat from the bedsheets kept the mind thinking.

We move in cycles as people, from top to bottom, through many lifetimes and lucky geography later. But, there are no Americans to discover, and finally, on the backs of survivors, some lucky "feudal" men and women will be able to stem the chaos that will ensue. As Sartre said, a predicted "Reign of Terror" will befall us. Politicians rise and then get slaughtered. Mainly, hoarders will be carried off or shot when found.

"It was only two years of this," he said, "but what were people's transitions? I only saw my adaptation and opportunities. The whole picture was too much to take."

We saw these stories from the heroes' eyes; we never saw ourselves as extras, the cast-offs in a film about someone else's life.

A CRY FOR HELP

<u>*September 15, 2020*</u>

The air is worse than it was yesterday. I want you to publish that poem I derived from your words as a collaboration, but it feels like *Grand Theft Auto*. People are running around killing each other. There's no morality. The ash wafts in like made-up memories derived from porn and gangsters. What's next on the list of experiences? Hacked. Broke. Permanently unemployed. Fu#k pension and retirement. I do cardboard boxes and ride out influenza, the social life of coke bottles for urine, and plastic bags for the big stuff.

Thank God for dog parks and those bag shoots. I look for cotton, anything. It gets most of the squish. The trick is to move only a little. Everyone knows your address once you get up from the makeshift card table. I do my shopping at night if you get me. The guy two tents over has a collection of bicycles that reminds me of those rich guys who collect cars. Why would you collect cars? Don't people know women can't tell the difference? A car or even a bike for a homeless person wastes time. There's gas and insurance, not to mention a driver's license required to drive one, and both just get stolen. It's better not to have anything. You call attention to yourself.

Life is a whim. I constantly feel hungry. The guy next to me eats the same canned soup over and over. Somehow, he got a case of it and kept it outside his trailer's door.

People like us don't take hand-outs; we sit here. I am telling you, much land is available for people experiencing homelessness. The other day, I saw a man in a wheelchair in a dry, reedy area near the airport. We start forming shantytowns, making trades in stolen goods, and even laughing. I admit it sounds like hyenas in captivity. Out of nowhere, and for no reason, people laugh. It's loud, like a car alarm audible, and you know exactly where it comes from. It's fear.

THINGS WILL GET BETTER

September 16, 2020
These possible lives, Fleury and Jaggy's,
When Ken came from SF empty of shoes,
His short opera began without voices
But muttering,
About lightweight virgins with
Pink vulvas: puckered mouths.
You could not misplace them,
Simply because that's all you wanted to see,
Drooling dolls lined up in ballerina slippers
And spandex, primarily gray,
As if the whole event of my gawking
It was morally depraved.
Oh, and you mentioned how they were all Asian.
The slightest and most petit waif
Without any notice except that even in their
Seeming innocence, they judged me.
Everyone was pirouetting in a
Line I could not cross even if I wanted.

Neither of us can afford anything
But an utterly willing person,
And even so, they have to be naive.
We might last one date,
And then we thumb through our wallets,
Eyes glazed.
I feel liable:
Checking AdultFriendFinder.
Women from London and Temecula,
But this woman from
Danville has yet to get back.
Mid-September is here.
It's the 13th.
I feel great, delusional.
I worked one day this week.
I recorded several compositions, but I ran out of
Memory.
They disappeared like all the women.
I even sang with the microphone and
Portable speaker as
The stereo speakers
We were playing "Right Here."
I am feeling better about my voice.
A perfumed blouse. I remember.
I walked behind a woman with no butt,
And she smelled of cheap perfume.
I can't place it. It's a classic scent.
I had a piece of meat last night—chef's graces.
I would love to travel by car with friends.
We wouldn't even have to drink.

I would love to go to bars or
Places along the way and play
Music and sing.
I was trying to sing opera.
I may try to record myself.
It must be fun seeing Asians coming to work.
You have your own at home.
There should be no bitterness,
Just a kind of knowingness.
Women are just people, aren't they?
Without our minds a scurry
Are they covering their forms?
Sex seems to be this recurring theme.
I want to have sex more than eat.
But I live in so much sand,
And now smoke.
My music satisfies me.
I am recording it in 24-bit.
I have no bitterness, per se,
And that's because I am avoiding reality.
I know I have to pick up another job, at least.
I don't look forward to it.
I was tied down to an empty formality.
I have no audacity,
And that's because I don't know what
That means.
When they started off-shoring,
I knew we were going under.
We keep wanting other people to do our work.
I slept almost eight hours last night,

And no artist should ever marry,
But he should be with women who inspire him.
And things will get better.

WHAT IS GOING TO HAPPEN?

<u>*September 20, 2020*</u>

Tonight, I noticed an older woman with arthritically deformed hands and back. Her hair was stringy and greasy. She had sacks in her shopping cart, and she was perusing slowly. It struck me that she must be struggling. I worked three days this week and one day the week before. I can't imagine what she is doing for money, but she could be a millionaire for all I know.

So, I bought a package of marinated chicken and a value pack of steaks and gave them to her when she came out of the store. I asked if she could use some food, and she said yes. I told her I did not cook them to ensure she had somewhere to go and that I had just bought them in case she hadn't noticed me in the store.

She reminded me of my mother, who died a few years ago. I saw her eat little throughout her life and always had uncovered paper cups of food she apparently would eat later. At a point in time, I realized she might not be doing so well, except at that point, she was also in an independent living situation, where they fed her three meals. So, that must not have been the case. I remember getting her things to make a smoothie, but I couldn't keep it up. I felt horrible later on. But you don't know what parents or older people are going through because they never complain.

Then, when I got home, I heard that on October 1, 74,000 airline employees would be laid off. I need another job because as these jobs dissipate, the competition for existing jobs will grow even more intense. My industry is related. While moving through the grocery store, there were many spaces and few representative products. I remembered that in the meat-packing industry, many people have COVID, and the prices for meat are unbelievable. I bought a huge container of blackberries, and they were all spoiled. I looked at the back, not under the label. I just threw them away. I didn't want to go back and argue.

I sensed that September would be a telling month, but maybe October. We must act quickly before the economy returns; perhaps it won't. I can watch Netflix every night if I have to, but I am still determining if I can afford to eat. I had my meal for today. What is going to happen?

ON BROADWAY

September 22, 2020

I started with several improvised contemporary classical piano solos on Broadway (4270 Broadway Oakland, CA 94611). Then I sang about five songs; I wrote lyrics and sang over International composers' works. These songs were from collaborations specific to SoundCloud, but I took them out and did them on the steps of a high school. Traffic passed, and people listened from a Bluebottle takeaway across the street; a woman walked her dog. I asked a young man what he thought of my music. He said it was "Pretty good."

I am curious to know how many listened. My head was down, mostly trying to listen to the points I had to put the words into the air. The sound system, a Bose S1 Pro, sounded great, taking in the iPhone-directed SoundCloud music and my microphone. It was tough at first. I am shy. I did most of the songs at least twice to practice. Tears sometimes came to my eyes because it was an old dream and a knowingness that I had ignored pursuing until now. The words are also sad at times. I wish I were never so frightened of expressing myself in public, on a soapbox, but I lost my confidence when my father died. I went from positive to negative when I saw my relatives wearing sunglasses in our apartment. I cried in the bathtub until the bathtub was dry. These songs come from my soul. That's all I have that's worth anything, and my purpose is to be myself.

"LOVE COMES AND GOES WHEN IT WANTS"

Yes, it does with an unevenness that even embarrasses those who cannot. I have been with both parties, so I understand it to the point of refraining from any intercourse. The lack of words always disguises the tumultuous insides. If I shared them, I feel a woman would be appalled. The desire to penetrate and lap up liquid is base. In the exact motions of an apex predator on top of a gazelle with my teeth on her neck, blood leaks; her eyes open but remain empty. The drive seems to negate the possibility of life—the scarcity of opportunity. The distance from water, the fact of every predator looking for honey, it turns into a death match: The ultimate Gladiator, the last one standing, and mostly you understand how you can't measure up in the long run and that the woman won't want you, body, money, job, and words, because you didn't use them in the beginning as a means to communicate. It ends as quickly as it begins unless you cannot avoid the instinct to take everything at the first chance and promise her that you want this to last. I want this to last. I like myself. I can pick you up. Are you as willing as I to accept a person, not a God? I don't want to be a God. I want to be me.

SORROWFUL

October 22, 2020
This time, I mention you,
Sorrowful,
Out to the furthest bell in the sea
The skylight falls beneath the Earth
And everything is still.
Waves barely beat upon the
Surface, their light little smiles
Disappearing in the dark
Their bodies were slightly rolling in the sand
The mood is turning light into dust.
The fires are burning, and most of us
Can barely breathe.
I reach out to you,
Can you hear me?
Somewhere in the night, I call.
Somewhere in the night, I whisper to you.
Somewhere, I think of you.
The sea leaks out
Then, he comes back,
Over and over.

You'd think our lives would change,
But they do not.
We were put here to work and
Not complain.
But the work we do is beautiful.
It is teaching others of the Earth to be.

*Sorrowful (Lyrics by Mario Savioni over Ashot Danielyn's 'Dark Sorrow' music)

THE HUMMINGBIRD

November 19, 2020
It would help if you met my hummingbird,
Is he aggressive and, therefore, alone?
He will not perch on my hand
Because he knows I think he is delicate,
A Pushover, which is an entirely different bird.
But he runs his beak through other
Birds all the while
And wastes the water.
There is more than enough for them.
Why was it one day that seven of them together
Were drinking on the feeder, and
Otherwise, was it just him?
And why do I assume it is a "he"?
It could be a woman.
The women I know are
Violent, vindictive, and opportunistic.
Each thinks I am a pushover.
Instead, I am a Titmouse, and in a mirror,

I am constantly
Thrashing my head against the glass,
To the point that blood comes from my beak,
And I have a headache.
Neither do I hear the woman who loved me.
She could not stand the futility of my life.
I am still looking for the mirror
Its owner removed it to protect me.
Each season, I return to find it.
The owner has put two large ones
On either side of the balcony,
So, I must choose which one to operate,
But it is too challenging to be in two places.
Luckily, there is a limit to my vanity;
I am older now.
Instead, I fly in circles and have learned to sing.
I am singing to find love, but as I said, I am older.
The sound doesn't even attract predators.
They sense something is wrong.

MOTHER'S LAMENT

November 26, 2020

Perdita Marie Swift, b. Jan 6, 1930 — d. Aug 1, 2018

The following is a poem I found the night before Thanksgiving. My mother died in August two years ago. I never knew she was alone this way; I figured she was a typical mom, but she was not. My father died when I was ten. That left her to raise two children alone, and she hadn't worked for at least ten years taking care of us before he died. They were divorced. She never had a stable job for the rest of her life. Her marriages were relatively short and fraught with unhappiness. Husbands took care of their wives in those days. Her husbands, after that, were drunks or inferior employees.

The sadness of her isolation spills over me. Our parents are not "normal" people. They have sacrificed themselves for us, although that's a cruel burden. Still, I would have had her live with me the whole time if I could. But, I lived in small places, and my job as a server barely supported me. She had Alzheimer's and would wander off or forget to turn off the stove. She would fall on the way to a nanny job for which she wasn't qualified. She would fall on her way to a cafe, where she would sit for hours when she was in a shared home. She would fall into the bathtub because of dehydration. She hated and never drank water. I tried to lift her, but she was too heavy. The ambulance would come. Her mother died alone when my mother was 18, and my mother's father died when she was two. Her brothers lived with her mother and were pages at the Supreme Court. My mother lived in foster homes because her mother couldn't support her. It was during the Depression. Her uncle raped her, and so did her boss. My mother was a runway model on television, a commercial artist, and dated San Francisco Mayor Moscone. I found the following poem: the italicized section toward the end written by hand in pencil and pen; she typed the rest.

Oh, my son, my daughter, I miss you so.
Where are you, what's happening, what's new?
It's been so long since your Daddy died
And I miss him too.
Once, I bribed a friend to give you
A ticket to come to see me, so many miles
From home. I was sick and sad, and all you
Did was hold my hand for just a second, then
Off with your friends, you ran.
In a week, you were gone.
I can't remember what you look like;
It's been so long.
Are you happy? Are you strong?
All those times, I helped you out with one thing
And into another,

Hugged you tight when there was thunder.
Son, you said you'd take care of me when I am old
If only you knew that time is now.
You will never read this poem,
But other children will.
One Christmas at the airport, I took you both aside
And said, "Can't we three always plan to
Be together
At least at Christmas?"
You got married; I disapproved.
Because she was taking me from you
Cause she wasn't right with you
I never interfered, though you were getting hurt.

BY EXAMPLE

November 29, 2020
I prefer not to have to take people anywhere,
Unless, of course, they are that ex-girlfriend
With whom I am still crushing.
I want to take her somewhere quiet.
I left her as she was.
She had to change if it was ever going to work.
She pretty much said, "Goodbye."
And I knew I couldn't change her,
Nor did I want to.
She was perfect in my eyes,
Made of the entirety of perfection.
Her eyes, nose, teeth, chin, cheeks,
Ears, hair, neck, shoulders, arms, hands,
Elbows, chest, and all that implies.
Her waist, back, butt, front, legs, feet,
How she spoke,
What she said,
And how she looked at things was enchanting.
She was my dream, and I was not even
Fireworks on an arbitrary evening.

She remains a fixture in my imagination;
I am lost in her example,
And I will never recover.

SPREAD FREEDOM

December 1, 2020
Spread Freedom
Linked to sorrow.
Nightingale mourns
The moon's a sparkler
In the sky.
Somber moments
Chill the air.
Fortune stirs the
Cleverest among us.
We partake of
The gentle season's smile.
At night,
We stare into
Each other's eyes.
I travel with you through the trees.
Into the snow, our shoes sink
To curb our progress,
But angels are due
To sit with us,
In the clean air.

We expect Angels to survey
The state of affairs.
We know where we stand.
We stand together:
Facing the truth
Facing the sky
Facing the sun
Facing each other,
And knowing the way.
We are in unison.
We are true friends.
We are friends, indeed.
The long-awaited attendance
To our needs.
We are free
We are free
Free to be.

HEDGING BETS

December 19, 2020
"More surface," I must be a rapist
Wanting to dry-hump your words.
"To the sky today,"
I look up to you,
But not as a friend,
But as a frenemy,
Which sees the beauty you possess,
And jealous of your pickiness.
You haven't worked for years
And the jobs I have done are beneath you.
You have a beautiful wife.
Her capacity to love you,
Just as I do,
Because I see my naiveté
Or is it purity
In you?
My body has nearly given up.
I sleep for a few hours and then wake.
There is no follow-through.
My body is on red alert.

It writhes, it's painful,
Muscles are tearing and literally
Both arms are separated
And their musculature is torn.
I can't sleep on either side.
To get any rest, I have to stay in bed
And try to fall asleep again.
I do this over and over until
It is nightfall.
The only thing I can get done
From time to time is run.
And when I run, I carry my
Body at an angle,
It's like I am pulling it:
"Please, please, this will help you."
I am fragmented. I am in pain,
And I feel like I might be dead by
Next year.
I shiver.
I ache.
And I have nothing to look forward to.
My job is going to run me into the pavement
Or I am going to get that virus.
It's like I am finally greeting that bear
In the forest.
There is just no language or argument
And you know how I argue,
I put everything into it.
How I play music,
Write lyrics,

Record myself singing.
There is just nothing left.
I see that I am irrelevant.
I thought I could see it all
And people would know
What I was talking about,
But there is no one listening.
I am in the forest alone.
I haven't loved anyone
For so long, I can't remember.
It was 1999 when I broke
With the Flight Attendant.
She stopped communicating.
Every woman I have ever loved
Is gone, and they were short-lived.
I spent my coins.
I have nothing left.
No ideas.
You say, "That's just a play of words."
"It's cold."
It's not that cold,
I am just weak, tired, and underfed.
You say "nearly everyone" you have
"Known is either
"A disappearance...or else an afterthought."
Like me, they are all gone.
I have dreams of people I have known,
Who were friendly, but they never really
Followed through.
They kept their distance.

And I think I know why.
Everyone is hedging their bets.
Like you, by the first of the year,
I will have to reassess who is still with me.
I don't blame them.
I am a screech owl.
I know those blackbirds.
We have them here,
And I feel like they know
We are all going to start eating each other.
The feeding is going to be good,
"Just watch," they say to each other.
Do you remember when we saw those
Birds here?
There were hundreds of them on
The electric lines.
I agree that as the depression hits,
It will force us to move,
To try to make some living wherever we can find it,
But it is going to be different this time.
I feel like we are going to drop to the bottom,
From first-world nation to fourth.
Insanity will overcome us.
In our desperation.
"Plagues of thought gone under by dawn."
You say it so well.
I don't have the words anymore.
Things are too desperate.
For me to wax nostalgic.
You watch James Turrell.

Attendance is down, so
You have time to write.
I am so glad you got more Bolaño.
Yes, you have a month off too!
It's like this cruel gift.
We have, as you say, to
Create "imaginary platforms."
Upon which to move our social lives.

BLOOD RED OF
THE WATER

December 20, 2020

Blood red of the water surrounded the sailors, who had never sailed nor knew how to swim.

Paint is like water running over a boat, which seems to be shipwrecked. The people have capsized. The ship, rendered by human hands, is a living thing cobbled together for a painting to create the best composition. It becomes what we look at to garner catharsis in a museum, where the privileged shuffle, immune to the disaster that is coming.

You are supposed to see yourself in art. Even this Titanic is only beautiful to those who have never sailed and never left a dead-end job. Capitalism, or man's inhumanity to man, is sucking the air. Everything is two-dimensional, a photograph, a memory, not what life should be. It is stark raving mad, a dog that has overeaten and can barely go outside.

Cityscape with empty migrant vessels. New World Order. The crossing for those who would not accept them will remind one of a cemetery. The sky, like in the Industrial Age, is sedimentary. Each landscape is like a Whistler rendering.

The Ark is under construction, except that the world isn't clean. It is a hollow vessel in the planning stages. The shadows of its ribs show no hostages.

I was envisioning the journey of the immigrant. The empathic water looks up at the edge of a boat full of migrants, not knowing anyone in particular, but like a shark getting a sense of appetizers. The sardine can soon spill over and reveal the fish. No one belongs in open water.

This luscious swell, out of focus, heaving, hiding, consuming, indifferent but ominous, is like the vision of an immigrant who has lost his glasses in the escape from horror only to be met with frightening uncertainty, stuck counting waves that seek to steal him like a sheepish coyote.

The wave floats like an empty holocaust that is the White House, dried to the bone, hollow, and in a storm.

The simplicity is haunting. It goes to the very essence of things, our childhood conception of reality, a kind of scientific short-handedness, the stroke of a child, which we have never left as the first grace of our being. The stool, too, is reminiscent of kindergarten. You no doubt take advantage of the light in this otherwise darkened room. Oh, what a great plan. What a superb rendering of the ocean, mountain, or vista, which is always the landscape of the human psyche. We seldom study the background. Isn't it almost always out of focus or scurrilously considered? And yet, to be aware of it might wake us to our self-centered views. It could be anywhere. We could be anywhere, and our genotype is the same. I want to hold you like the dolls in the attic and get back to that first dream. Who we are is in storage, brought back to the table and chairs. We danced around as children, learning to treat each other as human beings.

FOREST FOR THE TREES

<u>*July 26, 2021*</u>
The world comes through Boston.
The "O" in Boston and the other "O"
Let it all in,
And so do Harvard and Boston College,
And all the other schools
From the Union.
In fact, through the Bostonian leaves,
We judge the Tree,
See the light at the other end of the tunnel,
How a house might be seen,
A view in general.
I drink my cup of Joe
To your suggestion
Stamped on my mind,
Like a waiter in a cafe
Juggling the process of preparing
And bringing food,
Taking orders,

And maintaining a positive emotional charge,
So that everyone is pleasant,
Despite his view, in general,
Because he sees the forest for the trees.
Lost to themselves,
Some wearing masks,
Some naked,
In contradiction.
There is some beauty, however.
If COVID takes them out,
They never took science seriously anyway.
It's a numbers game.
Nobody's going to tell them anything.
"Boxes," eh?
I paint in the air with the notes from my piano.
Today, for example,
I improvised six piano works,
While at Powell BART station,
Which was practically empty,
I sang at least seven songs.
The police came and said that
I had to wear a mask,
And not to trip the blind man
Who just happened to appear.
One of the cops, the "bad" one, said
He could have given me a misdemeanor,
That sounds like a noogie.
I get the sh#t they dish.
It's like I am a 61-year-old man
Improvising piano compositions,

As if I were Erik Satie himself,
But none of that gets noticed.
Nor does the cutie in blue jeans and
A white sweater
She is having problems putting more
Money on her
Clipper Card.
Ever consider that all of this is
A la Minute?
I mean, there were, like a
Thousand people going by,
Whole bunches of kids from schools,
I felt empty.
Invisible--
Why artists are poor.
Half the country is praising a fat white man,
Who spends $130,000 on sex with a porn-star
Then denies it.
You are either proud or not.
Make up your fu#king mind!
She said that when she saw him
In his underwear,
She knew she was going to have to do it.
The idea of that guy in a pair of boxers,
Black socks and dress shoes,
Trumps any image with a
Tendency to make me throw up.
It's just like knowing when your child
Has pooped in his diaper.
Any hope of the thin veneer of a filter

Is gone.
Impressionism becomes a cock fight.
Between monkeys throwing
Feces around the room.
No man is a banana.
He's a "vibration from Laurie Andersen's
Table-sounding sculpture."
On the third floor,
Which used to be a fancy restaurant,
You mention Glenn Kaino and Brian Eno, too.
You are moderating the passage of visitors.
You say it may rain.
You want a shower.
It's lights out.
You don't have to wear a mask.
You mention Eno's "Sustained Heaven."
I clearly understand.
Everyone is equally pulled.
By the same blanket of the foreign
Power that invented COVID,
Then, set it free.
I heard in a movie last night
That everything political is planned.
I walked through San Francisco today, and it
Was empty.
Where are the millions of
People on Wednesday?
I played to silence.
I played to the emptiness.
I told myself, via an article that said confidence

Was king in getting the attention of a female,
That I was going to sing like I was good at it.
Of course, I sat against the wall and didn't
Look at anyone.
I am glad you are taking ten days off.
You mention the woman you see.
It would be best if you didn't do dictation.
It's a recording of your mind,
And that can get you in trouble.
Ah, but you aren't dictating anything.
The phone is listening to your conversations,
How the CIA listens to dialogs.
It records all our weaknesses,
So when we line up in front of the gas chamber,
The records will be read,
And you'll crack some dark joke,
As if humor is a salve.
And it is.
You rub it all over your skin,
And it keeps the Eczema at bay.
Later, you say that the rain did come.
There was drought,
As if California wouldn't know what that's like.
I am glad the garden was beautiful.
I imagine some rich person owned it first
On the backs of the workers.
I talked to a couple who used to be in
Hollywood and would print and process
Stills for the studios.
One was an investor,

And the other was an architect.
Their child washes dishes for a living
But just finished a novel.
We laughed.
I only thought of it later that he should
Read Richard Wright's *Black Boy*.
Wright describes a White server,
Who needed her apron tied.
"Oh, Richard," she said, "Can you please tie this?"
To which Richard was stunned.
Those ties were like rattlesnakes.
He wouldn't dare be that close to
A White woman.
But she trusted him.
Can you imagine how articulate he was?
How brilliant!
Hell, I would wash his dishes and
Clean his shoes.
I would look into his eyes and tell him,
"White supremacy."
Fu#k that!
Stupid White folks!
Their actions and words are their indictments.
They are as dumb as...
I love that the neighbors are dropping by,
The birds are singing.
Knowing my hummingbird, however,
Is to understand birdsong.
It's just like a drunk trying to seduce a stripper.
Let the temperature rise.

It means I can wear shorts and
Running shoes at work.

THE WHITE DRESS*

August 1, 2021
An apology.
Observing is not enough,
Nor are they not doing anything.
Both seem ominous against the worry
And contradict each other.
Why would a man harm a woman?
She screams,
Yet, in the foreground,
Her body is already broken.
She lies in a dream,
In a clearing.
A man plunging a knife,
Pulling her entrails.
Is she both lying and running?
The murderer ceaselessly represents a mother,
Who holds her hands, seeking forgiveness.
The family never stopped identifying
With the tapestry of death.
As a "family heirloom," the body flees
Ordinary unhappiness.

Humiliation is what women face.
Men make them submissive.
Domesticate them.
But women want babies.
And men only want women.
Men are dissatisfied with themselves.
Melancholic.
When someone doesn't love you,
It is pathetic to grieve.
Get over it.
The murderer stole her gaze.
Her interest was to stop the violence.
To address men's anger.
"We never stopped identifying
Armed horsemen...."
The young artist confused art in life
For him, everything is chaotic,
He idealizes
But violence is the same.
It's humiliating,
Pristine,
Dusty.
With the name, things are always complicated.
It just resides as majestic nonchalance.
She died when she was 33.
Hitchhiked.
Solitary,
In a wedding dress,
Performing,
Articulating something true,

A declaration of love or a work of art?
Alienated by the female condition
Sometimes, making something leads to nothing.
The entire story you want to tell
Must be contained in a minute.
The artist must immerse herself in her anxiety,
Sacrifice everything.
What is a person prepared to do to be loved?
A man eating his lunch
In the middle of a junction,
With impeccable ceremony:
Cutlery, a white tablecloth,
And a car is just missing him.
Abramovic, too,
Dressed in white and sat on rotting flesh
Wiping the blood with her dress
She died from it, and her obsession
Always wanting to be loved.
Was she asking for it?
Found in a shallow grave,
Raped.
Strangled.
Unusual guest paying tribute to love
And peace
Was this part of the performance?
Stuck thorns into her,
Cut her throat,
Drank her blood
Tied her,
Whipped her,

Brandished a revolver
Risked the audience's treatment, where
Words are useless.
Some men go about their day
After raping and killing
Fritz in blood
Tired of war
Meets the mother of a dead girl:
The body that feels at home without regrets
Schemes of revenge
Evidence of sorrows
Abandonment
Wake of sadness
Debris of dead virtues
Shrunk, shame having been left.
Four children, no money, no job,
No power, bullied by a man who was
Not content with having left her.
Happy and guilty on a grand scale.
I never helped her
Crushing
Holds all the tears
The mistake of motherhood,
And an empty guy.

*Notes from *The White Dress* by Nathalie Le'ger

HEDGEROWS IN PARIS

August 1, 2021
As your waiter,
You are in an orange dress, brunette.
I am in a blue shirt,
With Mr. P.,
I listened to your poem on YouTube.
It was not known if you could fabricate the sky.
Something about a child's arm, I could not hear.
But I heard that a boy learned to
Walk with his grandfather,
That all people are not lost,
Or that water spreads,
And citizens celebrate,
And yes, we would,
Knowing you are now in California.
Protecting your infant,
While watching flocks
Moving to Nebraska.
You find your best meditation,

> While the tea steeps
> Consumed by myth
> Trusting what you see
> Where fields in photographs
> Proved their existence.

As you can see, I only went through it once. Your voice is confined, cautious, and timid, adding to the overall impression to take you seriously. You hide a lot under your hands. The words are spacious, almost disconnected, expansive, and likely to suggest ambiguity.

I remember the words on the side of the old Berkeley Art Museum by a poet like blobs of light, Buddhist thought, the kind that resides between ladder rungs.

You never quite knew what they were saying, but it left you thinking or feeling like the answer to an LSAT question, which only felt the most correct because you didn't have time to test it, and you didn't know the process to resolve it, so you went ahead.

It's like reading a complex book and not having a dictionary, so you try to define the unknown words in context.

But there is enough abstraction/ambiguity to say that you have me wondering. Telling me that I have to ensure I have seen all the words to understand what happened.

But it's late. I worked again, like the day before, when I met you. It's been nonstop. The breaks are only at the beginning, never in the middle. I didn't even remember to use the bathroom tonight and did 49 tables.

I have had a few conversations with people; I got to know you thanks to your friend. She's as bold as a lion tamer.

I know about the St. Mary's MFA Program. It would cost $16,000; I was considering it. But, as you can see, art makes me wait tables. I am so jealous of your study abroad in the UK. I once did a reading at Betty's Coffee in London.

I love how much you've done in the field.
The conferences.
The publications.
The readings.
I don't have the patience to publish.
You see that it's mandatory to develop a CV.
I like the "large paper pink bags."
Again, there is space between your sentences.
And I am not referring to distance.
Were you writhing on the pavement?
I don't think you wept when you were born.
You just looked on,
Keenly observant.
Speaking was not required
At the outset.
I like "pious."
Pious for you.
You then talk about being close to a god.
Oh, and "dead rivers."
That phrase makes me think of dry rivers.
I think I understand people who give too much,
Because their intentions are suspect.
To engender friendship,
To say that I know you by your words.
I want to be close to success.

I have tried to publish.
To write and sing songs.
I love your photographs.
Again, they are spacious,
Well-composed, beautiful colors
Complement each other,
Lonely, observational.
I know that green-trimmed house.
I have even been in it, I think,
Just down on Ashby from the hotel.
I like how you capture fragments.
I did that with hedges in Paris.
I can feel the Bay Area.
The silence.
The loneliness.

THE BOOKPLATE

August 24, 2021
The bookplate speaks of its owner,
Which shouldn't the book provide?
8/12/21, you say there was heat on the
Day that followed,
The day you were speaking,
Had the same temperature.
Today is 8/20/21.
Eight days later.
A dark sky complements the heat here.
Everything is the color of taupe,
What realtors recommend painting
Rental apartments.
The sun last night was orange,
Which, of course, is the color of the future.
I love dystopian skies.
But I don't like what is
Happening in Afghanistan
Or at work, where the
Company keeps implementing changes
That take advantage of workers during COVID.

Companies keep greedily
Making changes so they can make as
Much money as possible,
And they use corporate speak,
Like 'Talent and Culture'
Instead of Human Resources,
Or whatever name they used before that,
Always pretending to reinvent themselves,
As if we don't know what's going on.
They should call it "Slavery."
We literally can't wait until the weekend,
But we are so triggered,
Soulless, spent, tired, used
That we have no energy.
We sit at our desks and
Play the kind of solitaire that social media is.
It is an attempt to communicate,
But it's embarrassing.
Lonely and friendless.
The drapes are closed.
You say your clarity was affected.
I doubt that.
The "passive egoist" mid-August became.
The country splinters, breaks, disembowels,
And we both feel it.
Science cast to the wind.
Everybody's a novelist,
And I don't mean that in a good way.
Some of them can't even write.
They wouldn't know the

Truth if it landed on their head
Like something at a construction site.
There's no certainty
To speak,
No direction,
No ground, but that dusty stuff
I saw it the other day at the hotel
In the middle of practically nowhere.
My ex-girlfriend said she had
Driven down the road a bit from where I stayed,
And she said it struck her as just a
Town that people slept in,
But nothing else, people of color,
Just staring off into space.
My colleague said it's just a
Corridor for meth, from everything
Below California and to
San Francisco and Los Angeles.
That seemingly is the only groundwork laid,
Invest in the certainty of drug addicts.
Hopelessness is a sure thing.
Days pass
And they make no motion toward
Sexual release,
Assembly line of absence.
Fear is there.
The absence makes the heart grow fonder.
A generation's eternal struggle
That fades to black.
But I couldn't commit suicide.

I would take a job anywhere.
Even at minimum wage, because it is a place,
Where I was getting paid and
Learning something,
Meeting people.
Sometimes, I want to be a barista at Starbucks
Everyone comes through there.
I like the mad rush to finish a task.
To give someone something.
Represents rest,
A place to perhaps meet someone,
With whom you could garner a connection.
I love cafes.
Yes, we are more accessible,
Not having anything
To make us financially safe.
We are stuck having to adhere to some job
That brings in something to
Put food on the table
Even though it may not be exciting,
But I guess life isn't about
Making enough money
To get comfortable.
We aren't supposed to be comfortable.
We are supposed to be involved,
In the middle of something,
No rest for the wicked.
And yet, I am grateful.
I have everything I could want.
Tonight, I didn't try to make the best of things

And the woman I was helping kept saying:
"Where were you...We are hungry!"
Which made my eyes roll.
I was standing in front of her the whole time
And she didn't even notice.
She was in deep conversation.
A narcissist.
Men don't think of anything but sex.
And if there is something wrong with that drive,
Then, they feel like dying.
The eyes have it.
They see all that must be put away.
How everything has its place
And if everything isn't organized
We harbor a sense of the unfinished.
It acts as a distraction,
A weight,
An unruliness.
Eyes will always come into view.
And distract you.
I like to look at them until they pull away
Or scold me.
Once, as you say,
The connection was made.
But I don't believe we need anything more than
Food on the table,
And we don't need that much.
I think of you and me.
You both have something
I have never been able to achieve.

You are like artwork.
You need patrons.
Fools never get their due.
That's why they call them fools.
In 2016, we had yet to learn
How soon the end would come.
I told my friend Bejan that I saw the end
Much sooner than he did.
He said at least 20 years.
I said two.
Our time is no longer our own.
It has dislodged us.
There is a plan, and it doesn't include us
Unless we submit to every whim of those
Who control the world?
Our only hope is complete submission.
And then, if things turn out
We might make it
To the other side.
Our time is not our time.
We get paid to live in barracks.
To sleep close to strangers.
And there's not one iota of romance.

THE LAST BREATH

<u>*September 14, 2021*</u>
"High-society poet and GARDNER?"
In those times, I guess you made money
As a poet and for your gardening.
That affair with Woolf,
Now, that's something.
Both of you in your rooms,
Gender shape-shifting,
Passing through walls,
As if there were no barriers
For being a woman?
No glass ceiling,
Just one castle
And a flag
With the "V" out front
For vagina?
Andy Summers,
Spent his winters
In the jail of spewing the truth:
Reagan as God
The government-controlled by

Polluters, fossil-fuel extractors,
And religious fundamentalists
Unscientifically hostile,
Fiscally insolvent,
Worldwide hate for Americans,
Or just a few whose toys and money
Made them billionaires.
It started as long ago as the Afghanistan war,
When bin Laden cited
Support for Israel, US troops in Saudi Arabia,
And sanctions against Iraq as his motivation.
In 2011, they killed him.
On August 19, 2021, you wrote of standing
In a gallery.
Your wife and you
Saw a rainbow.
It's still the second summer with COVID.
People are far away, and you said,
Amazon takes advantage of this.
Magic is fleeting.
What is an "unnecessary" escape?
I feel like it applies to my having to stay
Here, as my car downstairs
Has a long crack across the windshield.
It constantly gets bombarded on the freeway;
Those asshole truck drivers
Know what they are doing.
The problem is, it wasn't a truck this time.
It was a Panamera,
Which was off-white and chrome.

I was watching its wheels
Move up and down in the wells
As the body was barely moving.
Just straight down the freeway,
Smooth as glass.
While I was having so much
Fun watching this car,
I heard a click,
But I didn't realize what had
Happened until later.
By the next day,
The line went from one side of the window
To a place above me and on the right.
I can tell it is moving
Because there are things on the
Windshield that the line passes.
I signed up for a house visit;
$626 to replace it.
It cost twice as much as it cost last time.
Then I had a Honda.
Now I have an Italian car,
Economy version — 2014 FIAT 500L Easy
That I bought in '16.
Mercedes didn't want it,
So they lowered the price by a thousand
Since I didn't buy it the first day.
At ten thousand, I thought it was a steal.
But all the FIAT dealers have closed,
And each piece costs a fortune
And they come from Italy,

Apparently, with an entourage,
Fly first class,
Imbibe in the most expensive champagnes,
And, well, caviar,
Which, of course, isn't "Italian."
And when they get here,
They like to tour.
I saw herds of FIATs in various states
Of disrepair in Berkeley.
I have a problem with the dual-clutch
That's a recall issue.
Good idea:
Close all the dealerships,
So you don't have to make good
On the inherent problems.
But the car has been fun.
It saved me since I have been remodeling.
It's not a small car,
It's the car on steroids.
You can almost sleep in it,
But, of course, it's not long
Enough or flat enough, and
Every elevation change hits
You are in a place that causes pain.
As a heart patient,
It's like getting massaged
By a gorilla.
I have tried it several times,
It is a rare form of torture,
And I never slept through the night.

The lights typically go out
Somewhere in the car, almost every
Two weeks.
I finally bought LEDs,
But the dashboard keeps saying
The lights are out.
The NAPA Auto Parts guy said
He thinks the lights are acting like fuses.
We will see. I like LEDs.
I have often complained about others'
LEDs as blinding,
But now I am the blinder.
It's funny how that works.
As if I were a billionaire,
I probably wouldn't complain
About billionaires,
Unless, say, we were playing
Poker,
And one cheated.
I am an artist; I prefer playing solitaire.
Dating is too much.
Yachts? What am I going to do with a boat?
I am afraid of sharks.
Sharks of all kinds.
Ivan Vladislavic.
He sounds like a guy you don't want to
Mess with in a dark alley,
But he is from South Africa,
With a Croatian origin.
He's an author, editor, and professor.

His books are postmodern in style,
Mixing history with symbolism,
And he doesn't look that dangerous.
What a title:
The Restless Supermarket or *A Labour of Moles*.
There is so much wisdom implied in a
Good title and humor.
It establishes an enigma
That you have to explore,
If you have any nerves.
I know people who have never read a book
Or gone to college.
There is so much certainty.
In their minds,
That is the case of my least favorite person,
He believes that he is correct,
And he wields that weapon,
Beating others with it
Each time, asking for
Forgiveness,
He thinks being an asshole is cool.
No, an asshole is a piece of shit,
Something so unsavory
Not only does it stink,
But it's toxic.
For someone with a claimed 148 IQ,
You have to wonder.
It's like billionaires —
The fact that they have money,
It makes them think,

They have a right to lord over you,
Stop paying taxes,
But they don't.
That's not the whole picture.
It's not sustainable.
Eventually,
People just get pissed
And storm the Bastille.
Oh, wait, they did that.
Just not for the right reasons.
Trump wants America to control the world.
Obama wanted the US and the
Allies to work together.
Now that I think about it,
We can't avoid making enemies.
Aren't we privileged?
Like that guy, I don't like,
He only sees the world on his terms.
No one else matters.
What I learned from COVID
Is that we went from the
"Me" to the "#MeToo!,"
To the Narcissistic generation.
Americans are full of themselves.
So full they can't understand why someone
Would want to flee their country,
And come to the land of opportunity.
I think the opportunities are growing scarce,
And it follows.
As the rich-poor gap widens,

Most of us fall inside.
I have worked, but I am tired.
I tried standing on one foot.
For 20 seconds.
The first leg was fine,
But then the other one,
And when closing my eyes,
I was wobbly,
Shaking like a curtain in the wind.
The article gave me five years to live.
At most 13.
I love that the rain falls.
In California,
We don't have that.
We've removed the word
"Rain" from the dictionary.
There's no point anymore.
Sun and oranges,
As I mentioned
In one of the other messages,
The olive trees looked somewhat peaked,
Dusty and still,
Like an older man after
A heart attack —
Rigor mortis in mid-air -
A George Segal sculpture.
And how was Albany?
And Delmar?
We have one in Cali.
It's like the other woody resort

West of the Mississippi.
You might see billionaires there.
I have met a few.
I am glad you are having drinks with friends.
I like that, especially when
I have a lot in common,
Not with your friends, but I might.
I meant friends like us,
Artists are lingering at nightfall.
And yes, the drastic change is welcome,
Necessary.
But, while I was running in the hot sun today,
I realized I am no Olympian.
I was so beaten,
I wanted to lie down in the dirt and say:
"Take me."
George Johnson once said that his
Doctor said,
"You know, George, your life is like a ball.
"The older you get,
"The more you bounce lower and lower,
"Until you don't bounce anymore."
I understand where this is all leading.
Your circle of influence gets smaller and smaller.
If you started well,
You know, like a Trump or
Some other slob,
You might have some money
And influence,
But even then, life kills you,

Our bodies are time bombs.
There's only so much time,
And then your eyes close.
Like you, I have no visibility.
I want to make an "Invisible Man" shirt.
So far, all my energy has been geared toward art.
The job was to get me to paint pictures
And write books, make music and lyrics,
Sing, and maybe one other ambition,
But, after seeing my mother's demise,
And how we threw away all her
Notes in magazines
Pages, napkins, brochures,
I realize our dreams are not the
Dreams of others.
Once we lose independence,
We should call it.
I would hate to have someone live for me;
Which is to be the most miserable job.
You are watching people
Die before you enter that period.
It's like there's not a damn bit of hope,
Because they don't get paid enough to
Enjoy themselves.
Each day of work is misery's dousing,
Of the poverty of death.
My mother starved herself.
Her throat was unable to take anything down,
Her voice was unable to speak.
She breathed hard, and her

Throat rattled.
Her eyes were vacant,
But aware.
She heard everything.
She had no way of telling me
What she was feeling.
You could hear liquid in her lungs.
I knew she was in pain,
But she had waited for me.
She died, and then the gray
Pigment crept from the tips of her
Fingers and toes
Covering her whole body.
She was gaunt, and her mouth was open.
I learned what life is like through my mother.
You have only so much influence and power.
And if it isn't the right kind of
Influence and power,
You are irrelevant.
The world is for the shit-heads,
The liars and cheaters.
She was innocent
And she was tortured.
Born in the Depression,
Lived in foster homes,
Her father died when she was two.
Her mother died alone when my mother was 19.
Then, my father died six years after
My mother gave birth to me.
My mother raised two children with

An artist's brain.
The world is no place for truth,
For beauty.
Please, do not direct your energy.
To art.
Run as far away as you can.
I can feel it coming:
The gray tint.
The peakedness.
The rattle,
No one has ever heard of me.
My dreams can never be yours.
They die with their last breath.

www.ingramcontent.com/pod-product-compliance
Lightning Source LLC
LaVergne TN
LVHW032339150726
843469LV00052B/2135